———————— ★ ————————

Although I couldn't see William as anything more than a troubled—and frightened—adolescent, I slipped the wrench into my purse before I locked the car. Then I knocked on William's door.

There was no answer, only the pile-driver bass and the thin whinny of a guitar, but all the lights were on, and I stepped inside. There were papers on the bed and lots of black-and-white photographs strewn about like dirty snow. There was some red, too, spotted on the bed and on the floor beside the chunky leather motorcycle boots that seemed too heavy and clumsy for the long, thin legs protruding from them. William lay sprawled on the floor with his head against a corner of the cast-iron stove that heated the place.

I caught my breath against shock and the smell of sweat and blood, then forced myself to walk over and put my hands on his chest. As soon as I felt his heartbeat, I jumped up.

———————— ★ ————————

"A palpable sense of rural claustrophobia informs this mystery..."

—Publishers Weekly

D1019705

JANICE LAW

A SAFE PLACE TO DIE

W★RLDWIDE.

TORONTO • NEW YORK • LONDON
AMSTERDAM • PARIS • SYDNEY • HAMBURG
STOCKHOLM • ATHENS • TOKYO • MILAN
MADRID • WARSAW • BUDAPEST • AUCKLAND

A SAFE PLACE TO DIE

A Worldwide Mystery/October 1995

This edition is reprinted by arrangement with Walker and Company.

ISBN 0-373-26179-9

Printed in U.S.A.

For Arline Tehan

ONE

THE RIVER WAS an intense silvery blue in the low sun, the shadows of the salt marshes outlining its banks, until the flow was lost in the Sound. Below the rail bridge, we saw boats crowded around a marina, then marshland dotted with geese and swans, before the Connecticut landscape again changed to suburban sprawl, interspersed with tidy town centers and the usual sheds, works, and warehouses that cling to rail lines. Harry looked out the window, occasionally making a quick sketch with a Conté crayon in one of his tiny notebooks.

I tried to decide if he was tired. He had insisted on stopping briefly in New York to see an exhibition of African art and had roamed the Met's long corridors with his usual enthusiasm, declaring the masks marvelous stuff, the carvings irreproachable by ninety-nine percent of Western sculpture. But the city had been unseasonably hot for early May, and even though I'd insisted on cabs, I thought he looked pale.

"River light," Harry said.

"It should be twenty-four carat with the price of property up here."

"I'll have to get out my camera."

"Tomorrow," I said.

Harry had suffered a heart attack in January. January first, in fact: some New Year. It hadn't been a severe attack, the doctor said, and Harry had escaped surgery and medical heroics for a cure of rest, fewer fats, weight loss, and long walks. He grumped about boiled potatoes, pined for cheesecake and chocolate, and professed to be bored by walking. His doctor said that feisty patients did best, which was a consolation, but making my independent husband toe the medical line was something of a struggle.

The ills of middle age had hit us both with a vengeance, and I had been almost as cheered as Harry when a small but very exclusive and prestigious Connecticut gallery proposed doing a retrospective of his graphic work. The letter came just after he got out of the hospital, and selecting and cataloging work for the exhibit, overseeing the shipping, and keeping up an enormous correspondence with the gallery manager had provided welcome distractions.

Of course, Harry had been determined to go to the opening from the first. The doctor had agreed, on condition that I went along to do the driving and generally keep an eye on things. I worked late for a week, then turned the shop over to Baby, a.k.a. Ms. Quigley, office manager and personal assistant, and to Mike Garrett, who handles our security customers. Everything had run efficiently during Harry's illness, and I'd learned that Executive Security, Inc., could tolerate my absence for a surprisingly long time. Though I had mixed feelings about that, I was looking forward to the Connecticut trip as a break in the convalescent's routine and as a milestone of his recovery.

"You're not too tired?"

"Who gets tired in galleries?" he asked.

"That's the spirit. But I know that they're having people to dinner, cocktails, the whole thing."

"Don't fuss," Harry said irritably. "I'll be fine. Don't keep on about me."

The train seemed to be slowing, and I glanced at the small shingled houses and sheds, at jetties with sailboats packed impossibly close together, at the evening brightness with its edges dipped in ink. The conductor called the station. "Here already!" Harry said, and stood up.

"Wait," I said. "I'll get the bag."

He frowned but sat back down, and when I put my hand on his arm, he gave a rueful smile. Harry had lost about forty pounds, down to 180 from 220. There was a bit more gray in his hair, but he still looked trim and fit—if you ignored his pallor and the darkness under his eyes.

"We'll have a good time," I said, and he smiled again, before hopping up for the carry bags the moment the engineer hit the brakes. I grabbed the case, which, from the weight of it, was stuffed with his art and photographic equipment, and followed him onto the platform. We were at a diminutive red brick station on the edge of a pretty cove. To the west the sky was red, the marsh grass against it, green-black; the platform, the station, and the faces of the departing commuters were suffused with rose. The air smelled of salt and car exhaust, and after smoggy, crowded New York, the cool evening felt good. "Ah," said Harry, looking around with satisfaction. "They used to call this the Gold Coast."

Below the short flight of steps to the parking lot, a woman began waving energetically. She was dressed in a flowered skirt and matching blouse and as we came down the steps she exclaimed, "Harry Radford! I'm Isabel Browning of the Gallery Guild. I feel I know you already!"

This was not surprising, since Harry had sent her several photos as well as a short biographical statement for publicity purposes.

"And Mrs. Radford?"

"Ann Peters," I corrected, and she extended a dainty hand. I put her down as an artistic groupie and was childishly glad that I was wearing my best silk suit.

"If we could go to the car," I suggested once the ritual pleasantries were over. "Harry is supposed to rest."

"Oh, of course!" she exclaimed.

"I'm fine," my husband said. "We stopped at the Met."

"That wonderful African exhibit!" Isabel Browning said. "Just marvelous. So powerful."

I cleared my throat and picked up the case. Harry took one carry bag; Isabel Browning collected the other and directed us to a cream BMW with seats the color of caramel. In it, we talked of Art. When Harry's friends get together they talk about prices, about the cost of supplies, about agents, galleries, and techniques. With devotees, we talk about Art and the Meaning of It All. I much prefer technique, but my husband likes to be doted on as much as anyone, and he's quite able to hold his own in the airy-nothings department. He and our hostess dealt with the Spirit of Africa. I admired the pretty shops, the well-tended public buildings, the park, the river, and the increasingly large and lavish homes, until we turned onto a short street that ended at an impressive stone wall and a manned gate house.

"We're having guests to stay, Davis," Isabel told the gray-haired man at the control booth. "Mr. and Mrs. Radford will be in and out over the next few days."

"Just be sure they register their car," he said, giving us both a subtle but professional once-over.

"Thank you, Davis," she said, and we rolled into a manicured compound with acres of chemically enhanced grass and professionally barbered shrubs. There were no fences or walls between the houses. Each large yard merged with its neighbors, so that the Estates at Branch Hill resembled a vast golf course with near-mansions in place of greens and a flotilla of expensive automobiles instead of golf carts.

"... long time," Isabel was saying. "Really one of the first planned developments, a community in itself. And perfectly safe. That's such a consideration with children."

"The whole area is fenced?" I asked.

"Oh, I forgot your professional interest, Anna. You'd have to ask Davis, of course, but I believe it's all electronic—above the wall, that is. The stone wall went with the original estate. It's one of the most distinctive features."

As she spoke, she turned into a wide driveway that led to a pale stone house of vaguely French inspiration: formal and unadorned, with glass doors and long, blue-green shutters. There were tubs of annuals on a graveled area in front, and some flowering vines espaliered up the side of the building. It was easily the prettiest house in the compound, and Isabel seemed pleased with our admiration.

"It was a guest house once. One of the few buildings saved from the original property. Some of the new construction is—well, lavish but overdone. If you know what I mean."

I thought I did. We'd passed several gargantuan Colonials and a variety of overscaled dwellings with massive garages.

Martha, the housekeeper, a short, determined-looking woman with gray hair wound in braids, helped us upstairs with the baggage. Our room was at the back, big and square with twin beds and toile de Jouy wallpaper where picturesque shepherds and milk-maids flirted under ancient trees and decorative bridges. One of Harry's smaller serigraphs hung, well framed, over the mantel.

"I hope you'll feel quite at home," Isabel said.

I assured her we would and said that Harry needed to rest before dinner.

"We won't eat until eight or so. Cocktails at six-thirty," Isabel reminded us, then closed the door softly.

"I could get used to this," Harry said, and flopped down on one of the beds. I looked out at the lawns and trees, the fine slate and tile roofs, the flagstone and granite terraces, a palatial expanse ending in good stone walls topped with the latest in security sensing equipment. Professionally, I had to approve: Executive Security, Inc., advised on electronic security devices, among other things. Paranoia has been good to me and, although I hate to say it, urban decay has enabled me to make a bundle. But this was remotest suburbia; beyond the wall, I saw woods. We'd reached the farthest part of Branch Hill's lines, yet tiny red lights glowed through the house, Davis was on the gate, and an electronic net sniffed the air and monitored its photon beams. This, plus stone walls, was more safety than I personally needed, but I was to discover that security was very much on the collective mind of Branch Hill.

We were eight at dinner, all dressed to the nines, though Harry held out against a tie. Besides us and our hosts, Isabel and Ken Browning, there were the Ursons. Sidonie was the director of the gallery. Bradley, her husband, was something in banking now and had been something else big on Wall Street before they moved to Branch Hill in search of what he called "a protected environment." Also in the Brownings' palatial living room was Alex Valon, a tall, thin, courtly insurance executive for whom I'd worked several aeons before. That case had been a tricky one, and its conclusion, if intellectually satisfying, had not pleased his insurance giant, Independence Mutual. I hadn't had any work from Mutual since, and I'd lost touch with Alex Valon.

"Anna, what a very pleasant surprise."

"For me, as well. I'd heard you'd retired. I'd imagined Florida or Arizona."

"Just for the winters. Dottie flies, of course, but I take the train down." I remembered that Alex had been the poorest of poor fliers, a martyr to the shuttle and to corporate jets out of Hartford.

"And your wife? Is she keeping well?"

He made a little gesture toward the other side of the room. "Well enough. We live with our daughter and our grandson here. It's good for her to have some oc-

cupation. And then, these houses are enormous—
plenty of privacy."

"I didn't know you knew Alex." Isabel Browning
appeared at my elbow.

"Alex and I share a deep, professional interest in
chicanery," I said.

She looked a trifle nonplussed. "Oh, I was forget-
ting. Alex has become such a part of Branch Hill it's
hard to remember how recently he's arrived. Absolutely a bastion of the musical community! There's
never been a fund-raiser like him."

"A reaction to all those years of saving Independence Mutual's cash," I said and winked at Alex.

"Now, you must meet Sidonie Urson right away!"
Isabel said. "She's been longing to meet you!"

I thought that unlikely, as at the moment she
seemed to have cornered my husband. But I repeated
how pleased I was to see my old friend and followed
Isabel across the room. We stopped beside a glass table loaded with canapés so that I could meet Dottie
Valon, a small dynamo with bright, protruding eyes
and a great line of nosey questions. Fortunately, I was
in Isabel's capable hands, so Mrs. Valon's interest in
"some of the cases you and Alex worked on" had to
go unsatisfied. Her noisily vivacious daughter Cynthia was there too, in earnest conversation with Bradley Urson, a tall fellow with rather small features and
a lot of well-styled blond hair.

"It was so good of you to come. Cynthia has to run,
poor dear, but she stopped for cocktails," Isabel said.
"Like everyone else, she was just dying to meet your
husband. And you, too, of course."

"Of course," I agreed and shook hands with Cynthia, who gave me an indifferent glance and returned to Bradley.

"Marvelous," he said. "You know, this is what I consider creative fund-raising. The gallery's share is already earmarked for a number of significant projects in town."

"Bradley's in just everything," Isabel said vaguely.

"Youth work, mostly. Absolutely vital for the future."

"Absolutely."

"Sidonie!" Isabel grabbed my arm and waved her free hand. "Sidonie, don't set anything up until you've talked to Anna. She's made the rules very clear: no driving for her husband."

"I can pick him up any time," Sidonie said after we'd been properly introduced.

"Sidonie just *lives* at that gallery," Isabel said. "She's made it the most extraordinary success."

"It certainly has a wonderful reputation," I said.

She flushed. "I can't claim all of the credit for that. Frank Gerson picks the shows. I'm still very much on the business and management end."

"No gallery at all without business and management," my husband said gallantly.

"Well, there is quite a bit of work. But for a good cause..."

Sidonie Urson was a tall woman, elegantly slim with beautiful features and prematurely white hair pulled back in a knot. Unlike the gushing Isabel, she seemed genuinely interested in Harry's work, and despite her modesty, she appeared knowledgeable. She was discussing her ideas for hanging the works when two pretty girls wearing long, thin dresses came in and scooped up handfuls of canapés.

"Lindsay! Where are your manners?" Sidonie asked.

The girl who turned was pale and blond with good features and a sweet, rather shy expression. Her companion was darker but the same delicate type, with thin arms and legs and a similar mane of long, frizzled hair.

"A singer has to feed the voice," the second girl said. Hers was clear and low, despite the affected vowels. "This is the artist, I'm sure," she said, extending her hand to Harry.

"Good to meet you. You're—?"

"Angela Browning. And this is Lindsay Urson."

I'd taken them for sisters, but on closer inspection I saw the differences. Angela was in every way the original, the sharper copy, probably the leader. She was not as striking as her friend, having an assertive nose and a rather thin mouth, but she seemed intelligent and confident in a way surprising in a teenager. Lindsay, though physically graceful and more attractive, was clearly shy and awkward with adults.

"There you are!" Isabel exclaimed. "And barefoot."

"It's still warm. We were running on the grass," Angela said. "We're doing a song about grass. About lovers on the grass in spring. Very suggestive," she added with a glance toward Harry. "Not at all suitable. I won't let Lindsay see the lyrics."

"Heavy metal?" Harry asked.

Isabel Browning laughed a trifle uneasily. "The Madrigal Society. Positively a Branch Hill tradition."

"That's right. Guaranteed respectable. High culture gets away with murder," Angela said. "We're outta here, Mom. Good luck with your show, Mr. Radford."

"Have you had dinner?" her mother asked.

Angela made a vague gesture. "We'll call for a pizza when we're hungry. We might go to Lindsay's. If that's okay with Sidonie."

There was a flutter of instructions and arrangements, then Isabel moved off to chat with Dottie Valon and the two girls left, grabbing another handful of canapés as they passed.

"Lindsay'll be as fat as a pig," her mother moaned.

"She looks the lean type," I said.

"Diet. Angela, now, was born thin. Hardly fair."

"No?"

"Singers can carry a bit of fat. But Lindsay's a gymnast. Bone thin or no hope."

"How old is she?"

"Fourteen. Angela's a few months younger."

I'd have taken them for sixteen at least.

"Angela's a bit precocious. Talented as hell, of course. A real gift as a singer, but sometimes I think maybe too advanced." Sidonie Urson shrugged. "Of course, we have a fine school here and the kids get exposed to so much."

"One of the reasons we moved in," Ken Browning said, joining the circle. "Though how long it'll stay that way, I don't know." Ken was dark like his daughter, with the same pale complexion. In his case, it went with a large, square head, blunt and forceful features, and a mildly receding hairline. He moved very quickly and confidently like a man with energy in reserve, and he kept putting his hand on Sidonie's shoulder in a way I sensed she didn't like.

"Our kids' time, anyway," she said.

"Oh, our kids' time, sure. But the town's changing. Sidonie and Bradley are new," he said to me. "They don't remember when no one locked a door in Branch Hill."

"Coming from Washington," I said, "that sounds like once upon a time."

"Oh, Washington! Crime capital. But even here..."

Whether because of my business or not, Branch Hill residents seemed eager to recite suburban war stories. There actually had been a robbery in the estates the month before, and with a sage nod Ken predicted that a lot of his neighbors would be upgrading their security systems.

"Still, your crime rates must be low," I said.

"Not low enough. And there's a certain attraction for the criminal element," Ken said.

"The Dillinger Syndrome," my husband remarked.

"How's that?"

"Crooks go where the money is," Harry said genially.

Sidonie Urson laughed and assured him that the gallery, at least, had all the best in alarms and sensors; then Isabel announced dinner, and we all trooped into the dining room. I'd drawn a place next to Alex Valon, and he and I were soon deep in reminiscence. The table as a whole got interested in a fraud claim we'd worked on, and to my surprise, Valon proved an amusing raconteur. Then Harry was persuaded to part with some of his art-world anecdotes, which were a great success thanks to some discreet name-dropping. He had to repeat the crucial points of several stories for our host, who jumped up and down to help with the serving and the tidying up, and was in and out of the kitchen half a dozen times for more wine. I could see that the Estates liked its social life well lubricated, and I was pleased when I managed to get Harry upstairs and to bed soon after eleven.

"Not bad," he said. "Admit it. It's not as bad as you'd expected."

"I'd expected to have fun," I said.

"Liar. You expected they'd bore the pants off you."

"Our hostess has that potential."

"A charming lady. She thinks I'm a genius."

"So do I, but I don't believe in gushing about it."

"A little gush is good for the convalescent," Harry said.

"Right, but get to sleep. You promised to meet Sidonie Urson at eleven."

"She had some good ideas on hanging."

"Seemed to," I agreed, and put out the light. The room went black, then the shadows and the shapes of the windows emerged as the outside street and security lights took hold. The curtain moved gently in the spring breeze, changing the patterns on the wall and shifting the light over the mirror and the shepherds and Harry's serigraph. In the absence of D.C.'s omnipresent air-conditioning, I heard peepers, and I closed my eyes listening to their cheerful, monotonous songs.

A PHONE RANG in the darkness and I was awake instantly, although the double ring was distant and un-

familiar. The early nights of Harry's illness had con-
ditioned me: Any late-night call was bad, potentially
lethal. I was out of bed before I realized that I was in
a strange room, and it took a few seconds for me to
remember where I was. It was quarter to three. The
phone continued ringing as I felt my way around the
bed, but it stopped before I opened our door. Someone was talking in the room across the hall. ". . . just
hold on. But I don't think so."

The door opened, spilling light. "I'm sorry if that
woke you," Isabel said.

"Reflex action. I hope there's nothing wrong."

"Lindsay's not home. The Ursons' girl. I'm just
going to see if she stayed over with Angela. You know
kids," she added as she headed toward her daughter's
room.

I nodded sleepily and closed the door.

TWO

WE DIDN'T SEE anyone the next morning but Martha. Angela was at school. Ken was off to his work in the city, and Isabel had an early tennis lesson. Breakfast was laid out nicely in the dining room, and after coffee and toast, I left Harry with the morning papers, called a cab, and got myself to the car-rental agency. By ten-fifteen I had a mid-size Toyota, and Harry and I pulled up to the Branch Hill Artists' Gallery at eleven on the dot.

The gallery was a handsome old brick schoolhouse with a miniature Doric portico and a modern block and glass addition on the back. We had our choice of spaces in the side parking lot.

"Looks like we're here first," Harry said.

"That's odd. Though maybe someone dropped Sidonie off."

Harry got out and tried the door. It was locked, but a moment later, a figure appeared behind the glass. After a great fiddling with locks and bolts, a slight, nervous-looking woman with thin, fair hair pulled back behind her ears opened the door. "Mr. Radford?"

"Yes. I was supposed to meet Mrs. Urson today at eleven."

"Oh, come right in. I'm Georgie Cole. I don't know what's keeping her. Sidonie's always so prompt. She usually opens the gallery—especially when there's hanging to be done.''

Ms. Cole seemed upset, and I thought it best not to mention the trouble with the Ursons' daughter. Probably they'd been up half the night finding her and getting things straightened out.

"Don't worry at all," Harry said. "I've hung plenty of pictures. If we could see the gallery space—"

"Right through these doors. We keep the new wing for exhibits. The light's not so good in the older part, so we have the art classes there. In here." She opened a set of heavy double doors to a large, well-lighted room with a hardwood floor and tasteful museum-beige walls. The big shipping crates I'd last seen leaving Harry's Helios Workshop stood in a loose semicircle on a tarp. They'd been opened, and a few of the framed prints were unpacked and set against the walls. Otherwise, the gallery was empty.

"Ah," said Harry, "this is quite nice."

"Would you like a cup of coffee?" Ms. Cole asked. "I know Sidonie will be along soon."

"That's all right, we just had breakfast," I said. Harry'd already had his caffeine ration.

"I'll call Sidonie. I can't think what's keeping her."

"Maybe car trouble?"

"Oh, I don't think so. They have several cars."

"In the meantime," Harry said, "we'll see what we can do." He went over to the nearest case and began to lift out the works.

"Can I help?" I asked.

"Looks as if you'll have to. Or did you have something planned?"

"Not a chance. Shall I stack them or put them along the wall?"

"Let's put this lot along the side wall. I think the posters and larger things should be at the back. Even if we don't actually hang them, we can sort out where they're to go."

I spent the next two hours lifting and hauling pictures. Harry wasn't supposed to do anything strenuous, and the hanging process seemed to bring out his managerial, not to say dictatorial, instincts. While I held up each work, he stood at the back and gestured up or down, more to one side or the other, or waved the wretched picture off entirely and called for something different. I'd begun to think I'd underestimated his artistic temperament, when the doors banged open.

"I'm so sorry!" Sidonie Urson exclaimed. "I meant to be here hours ago."

"No problem," Harry said. "We're coming along all right."

"I'm gaining new respect for your profession," I said. "Is everything okay? Did Lindsay turn up?"

"Oh, you know kids," she said, but her face was strained and tense. "I'm sure it's nothing."

"She's not back." I knew the answer from the tone of her voice.

"I really felt silly calling the police," she said.

"But that's the right thing to do. You did call them?"

"Last night. This morning, really. Wee hours. I'd been so sure she was at Angela's. I didn't like to bother Isabel and Ken. I kept thinking, she's just forgotten to leave a note."

"Has this happened before?"

"Anna," Harry said.

"Sorry, professional reflex. But there are kids who—uh—wander."

"No, nothing like that." She ran her hand over her face nervously, and I brought over a chair.

"You'd better sit."

"No, I can't stay. I just came by to apologize and to tell you I'll try to get Frank over. Frank Gerson. He teaches at the college mornings or he'd be here now. He's good on exhibition hangings."

"I think we have things under control. What do you think?" Harry asked her.

Making a visible effort to concentrate, Sidonie looked around. "Yes, that's good. I'll get Norman, that's the janitor, to move out the crates and set up the partitions. How many do you think you'll need? They're six by ten."

"Hanging on both sides?" Harry asked.

"Yes."

"Let's say six."

"I'll tell him." She looked at her watch. "I didn't realize it was so late," she said, as another little wave of anxiety crossed her face. "Norman'll be finished lunch. Have you eaten? Maybe you could go out now; that way he'll have things ready when you get back."

"That will be fine," I said. "We'll get something downtown now and be back—when?"

"Two or two-thirty. I'll try to look in again. I know there's nothing really wrong," Sidonie said, "but with kids you can't help worrying. I'm going to make some more calls and—" she paused uncertainly "—and look around."

"Of course," I said. "We'll be fine, and we'll get all set up here. Don't bother to come back unless everything is okay."

"Oh, everything will be all right," she said.

Harry and I listened to the tap of her heels in the corridor. "What do you think?" he asked, his face serious.

"Trouble," I said. "That's what I think."

We ate at a health-food restaurant where Harry was guaranteed an assortment of low-cal, high-fiber, morally pure dishes, most of which depressed him. We discussed the show and his nostalgia for well-marbled steak, rare burgers, and ice cream desserts. Since my husband didn't want to linger in that culinary purgatory any longer than necessary, we returned to the gallery where Norman, a balding senior citizen with a great line of chat, was still busy in the exhibition space. We helped him clear the crates and held the portable exhibition walls so that he could bolt them together.

"A two-person job," Norman assured us. "Nothing to it, except getting the pieces so you can bolt them. I told Mrs. Urson that, but she went racing out. One of the kids sick, I think."

He looked like a key link on gossip central, so I nodded and said, "I guess."

"Kids," he said. "Something of an Urson specialty."

"Oh?"

"Sure. Bradley Urson, that's the Mister, is involved in everything youthwise in this town. Baseball league, summer basketball program, teen center. A pillar of the community in that regard."

"And Mrs.?"

"Mrs. is the arts. Strictly the arts. That angle right?" he asked Harry.

"A little this way. That's pretty good."

"Slots in the floor. Solid as a rock once you get them together. Yeah, the Ursons have divided the town between them."

"Useful people."

"Oh, yes," he said, but I sensed mixed feelings. "Course from a kid's point of view— Yeah, right in that slot. There. Hold your pictures perfect. From a kid's point of view," he continued, "could be a case of the shoemaker's kids going without shoes."

"Or the minister's wild sons?"

"Daughters in this case. Strictly daughters. Older girl's up in Massachusetts at college. Now, if you want to hold that door, I'll get the crates out of the way."

He slid the dolly away from the protective floor tarp, which Harry folded up and set on top of the crates.

"What day does the show end?"

"The twenty-first—three weeks from Wednesday."

"I'll have them back out of the storeroom first thing on the twenty-second."

"Fine, that's fine."

"Nice work," Norman said with a nod toward the walls. "Not like some we get in here." With this, he rolled away the crates. I went down the hall to open the doors for him, and when I got back, Harry was already selecting pictures for the freestanding walls.

"You get the whole history of the town?" he asked.

"I imagine that's an epic in Norman's hands."

"What do you think of the posters here? I've decided I want them separate from my other work."

It was nearly three before we finished, and three-thirty before we pulled into the Estates. Davis came out and double-checked our plate without a word of greeting, then waved us through distractedly. We had not gone fifty yards before two squad cars shot past us around the gently curving drives to a cluster of police and emergency vehicles at a wooded grove not far from the Brownings' house.

I turned into their driveway and had just put the Toyota in park when Isabel came out the front door. "Oh, Anna! And Harry! I'm so glad you're back. I was hoping you'd come. It's Martha's day off, and I didn't want to leave Angela."

"What's happened?"

"You saw the police cars?"

"Yes, what's wrong?"

She bit her lip in distress. Rotating lights, the ambulance, the police radio, and professional bustle had brought a glimpse of urban nights to Branch Hill's most exclusive enclave. "It's Lindsay," she said. "Remember, we got that call late last night?"

"Yes, yes, I know. We saw her mother today."

"They've found her. It's the most awful thing. They've found her dead."

"Here?"

"Yes. Right in the Estates. Just a few hundred yards away from our house, her house. She's dead. The police called to see if I'd go over to Sidonie. I've got to go, but poor Angela! She heard the call. She'd just come home from school."

"We'll stay with her," Harry said.

"Yes, if you would. I don't know what to say to Sidonie."

"Do you want me to drive you over?"

"No, I'd rather walk. I feel I need a minute or two." Isabel crossed the drive rapidly and started down the walk.

"We'd better go in," said Harry.

"You'd better go up and rest. I'll see if I can talk to Angela."

Inside, the spotless foyer smelled of floor polish and of the bronze chrysanthemums blooming in a big terra cotta pot. I glanced into the dining room, then the living room; both were empty.

"Up in her room, maybe?" Harry asked.

"I don't think so." I went down the back hall and through a butler's pantry to the kitchen. Angela was sitting huddled in a chair by the big square table, her face as white as Martha's spotless appliances, her large eyes enormous. I tapped lightly on the door and she gave a start. "Your mom went down to be with Mrs. Urson. She asked us to stay with you."

"I was frightened to be alone," Angela said in a small voice. Then, "Is it true?"

"There are a lot of squad cars and emergency vehicles. Yes, I think it's true."

Angela began to rock back and forth in her chair. "It's my fault," she whispered. "I should never have left her. It's my fault."

I gave Harry a look and suggested he put on some water for tea. He put the kettle on the stove and left.

"My husband has to rest," I said. "He had a heart attack this spring."

"Heart attack!" Angela exclaimed with a strangled giggle. "Maybe that's what this was." Then she raised her head and tried to sit very straight in her chair. She was dressed in a black turtleneck and a long black skirt, and it struck me that she was the only fourteen-year-old I'd known who could have worn such a costume. There was something theatrical but oddly dignified about Angela, even when she was half hysterical. "I'm sorry," she began, "it's—"

"It's all right. You've had a shock. Someone you knew well, your best friend—"

"Not my best friend," she corrected. "But we did a lot of stuff together because she lived in the neighborhood."

"Still."

"It was because of me," Angela said. Her control suddenly deserted her, and she started to sob.

I moved around and laid my hand on her shoulder, a little awkwardly, I'm afraid; I'm not the warm, motherly type. "Why do you think it was your fault?" I asked after a moment, without really meaning to.

"Because I shouldn't have left her, that's why!" She was nearly shouting.

"Where did you leave her?"

"Over at Scott's house. Scott Cushing's—over that way," she said, sniffling and pointing in the general direction of the professional-sized range.

"In the compound here?"

"Yes. It's the Valons' house. Scott's their grandson. I shouldn't have left her, but he's such a jerk. I got sick of talking to him." She began to weep again.

"Now, be sensible. You left her within a few houses of home? With a friend? How can you be to blame?"

"She was talking to Scott."

"And what time was this?"

"Just after nine. Martha was watching 'Mystery.' Martha says she wouldn't mind being as old as Miss Marple if she could look as good."

"So it wasn't late," I said.

"No," Angela said in a small voice.

"Do you often watch TV with Martha?"

"Oh, sure. We always watch the opera. We saw the whole *Ring*. Wagner is Martha's favorite. And we watch concerts whenever there's an opera singer on."

"Do you want to be a singer?"

"Yes," she said without hesitation, "but early music. Nothing later than Mozart unless my voice changes. Earlier would be better: Handel, Monteverdi. I love Monteverdi, but Martha likes a big sound. She says opera should be grand." Angela wiped her eyes.

"What about some tea?"

She hesitated. "I'd rather have hot chocolate. I can make the instant."

But when she got up, her hands were shaking so much that I took the packet and poured the water for her. "It's not your fault," I said. "You don't even know how she died. Even kids your age can have strokes, heart attacks and things."

Once again, I got the nervous giggle that was the other side of tears. "I'm sure it was a heart attack that killed her," Angela said.

THREE

WE HAD A VERY QUIET, tense dinner that night, just Ken, Harry, and me. Angela had eaten earlier with Martha, who had returned as soon as she heard the news. Determined and formidable, she swept into the kitchen, put her arms around the child, and said, "We'll be all right now." Her square face was closed, intense, almost unfriendly. "Angela will be all right with me," she repeated, and I knew I'd been dismissed. As I went out, I heard Angela start to sob again, and Martha's low voice saying, "It's all right, darling, it's all right." When Harry and I came down for dinner later, Wagner's swirling orchestration issued faintly from the back of the house; apparently, Martha's idea of soothing music was *The Flying Dutchman*.

"I must apologize," Ken said, gesturing toward the gourmet shop's catered dinner and Isabel's empty place. "She felt she couldn't leave. Sidonie's under sedation, of course, but everything's in an uproar. Bradley's been trying to get hold of their older daughter."

"She's at college?"

"Williams."

"It's a terrible thing," Harry said. "We're so sorry."

"I'm in shock," Ken said. He had a cocktail in his hand, and I noticed the flush starting to creep over his wide, square cheekbones. "And to have it happen here, practically on their doorstep. There'll be a new security firm when it's contract time—if not before."

"And is it clear what happened? Was it an accident of some kind?"

"Well, the police aren't saying much, but Isabel told me they think she was struck on the head. Several times." Ken looked down at his elegant seafood crepes. "They think she was murdered."

"Jesus!" said Harry.

"Do they have the weapon?"

"What?"

"A weapon?"

"I don't know. Isabel didn't have much time to talk. She said 'clubbed.' I think that was the word. She said Lindsay'd been clubbed with something."

"Any motive?"

"What the hell could be the motive for killing a fourteen-year-old?" His blocky face seemed to thin out with agitation, and I suddenly saw the lines of Angela's features. "It's some goddamn psychopath! The security company will find itself out of work!"

"It could have been a robbery attempt. Or a sexual assault," I said. "Those are the most likely with a girl that age."

"Nothing like that," Ken said abruptly. "She was wearing the same long dress she'd had on last night. No sign of anything—" Then, more calmly, "Isabel said it was awful. Lindsay'd been lying in the wood—just a cluster of trees, really. She'd apparently been lying there all night."

"How was she found?" Harry asked.

"That's bad, too. It was the Rosen children, Joey and Aron. They're—I don't know, Isabel keeps up with the kids' ages—maybe eight and ten. They were on their way home from school. The private day school has a bus that brings the kids right to the gate house. The boys took a shortcut through the grove and saw her lying in some leaves beside the path."

"A shock for them," Harry said.

"Do a lot of children use the path? It's odd no one spotted her this morning if the kids run through there."

Ken shrugged. "Some parents drive their children to school in the mornings."

"Grass would be damp in the mornings, too," Harry said. "They might stay on the sidewalks."

"Sidonie called here last night," Ken said. "I was a bit annoyed. If I'd thought—" he shook his head. "We could have gone out, searched—"

"There probably was nothing you could have done," I said.

"We might have seen something," he said. "Someone entering or leaving."

"That's what you have a gate for. But I imagine the police will be checking the security company's records."

"They've got to have something," Ken said. "Someone came in. Has to be."

I didn't say anything.

"Don't you agree? Who would hurt her here?"

"Hard as it is to believe," I said, "most murders aren't committed by strangers."

"There's never been a murder in Branch Hill. Never."

"Well, we'll hope for the best," Harry said.

"Harry and I have talked it over," I said then. "We'll make arrangements to leave tomorrow. With everything that's happened—"

"No, no," said Ken, sounding surprisingly distressed. "No need for that at all. Isabel wouldn't forgive me if I let you go. Besides, when is the opening?"

"Day after tomorrow," Harry said, "but surely it will be postponed."

"I doubt it. Everything will be set, publicity out— no, I doubt they'll postpone it."

"Even so," I said. "We don't want to give you more work. And I know your wife will be running back and forth to the Ursons'."

"All the more reason for you to stay. Listen, Isabel will be frantic about leaving Angela. I know I'll be nervous about having her and Martha alone in the house. God!" he exclaimed suddenly, striking the table. "This is why we moved out of the goddamn city. Strangers, violence, fear. I wanted to live somewhere where you could let your kid play outside. Where you could take a walk at night without risking disaster. No," he said more calmly, "you'd be doing us a favor if you stayed. You'd be in and out, and with more people in the house—"

"If it was a stranger," I said, "he or she should be long gone now."

"I know it's not rational," Ken said. "The fear's not rational. But you saw the state Angela was in. Tell you what, wait and talk to Isabel. See if she doesn't feel the same way as me. Okay?"

I looked at Harry.

"It's okay with me," he said. "Whatever will be easiest for you and your wife. I suppose we'll all have to be questioned anyway."

"Questioned? What do you mean?" Ken asked. He seemed genuinely surprised.

"Just routine," I said. "Did we hear anything, see a strange car, that sort of thing. If it was someone from outside the area, one of the neighbors might have noticed something odd."

"Oh, yes," he said, with a little self-deprecating laugh. "I wasn't even thinking of that. It's so unreal, you know. Like a cop show on TV. Not like Branch Hill at all."

"I'M NOT SURE," Harry said that night after we went up to our room, "that I'm ready to hear any more about Branch Hill."

"Or that special, privileged way of life at the Estates?"

"Especially that," my husband said.

From eight-thirty on, a stream of neighbors had dropped by to pool information. For a markedly uncongested neighborhood, news certainly traveled fast. But not as fast as the indignant rumors: the police chief would be fired, the security manager was already gone, the Estates ground crew was under investigation. Davis, the gate man, whom I'd heard praised to the skies the day before, had been asleep at his post; he was a drunk, a front man for a gang. To hear the Brownings' neighbors, the quiet and exclusive town of Branch Hill was under daily assault from the worst sort of criminals, and the Estates—an over-secured outfit if I ever saw one—had been negligently, even criminally, exposed. Nowhere was safe—that was the desperate undercurrent—and people who'd paid a high price for security were furious. And frightened.

In that atmosphere, it was something of a relief when Isabel got home. Isabel had the facts, and her white, strained face took us away from posturing indignation to real grief. She'd lost all the society flourishes and gush that had made her off-putting, and when she came in, she dropped into the first chair in the living room as if she couldn't walk a step farther. Her husband went over to the chest that held the liquor and poured her a whisky.

Isabel took a sip and a deep breath. "Where's Angela?" she asked.

"With Martha," her husband said. "They're deep in Wagner." The strains of the *Dutchman* were just detectable in the silence that had settled over the compound with the departure of the squad cars, the ambulance, the photographer's and police chief's and coroner's cars, and the dispersal of the news vans and reporters' vehicles at the gate. Davis, whatever his other sins, had been assiduous about keeping the media at bay. Deprived of access to the scene, they had contented themselves with shots of the massive walls, Davis's kiosk, and the stream of police vehicles, while rehearsing for us the dimensions, history, and value of the property beyond. There was a certain smugness about the resulting TV reports, a kind of racy enjoyment. If the deaths of the poor are ignored, the deaths of the rich are served up as a vulgar object lesson: *memento mori*.

Isabel sighed, but didn't say anything. A smothering closeness was not the Brownings' vice, and like

Ken, she seemed content to leave Angela to the housekeeper.

"Harry and Anna were thinking of moving out," Ken said. "But I told them it was no bother having them here. Quite the opposite."

"Yes," she said. "Please. I know I'm going to have to be at the Ursons'. Sidonie's taken it very hard."

"And her husband—Bradley?"

"I don't know," Isabel said and sipped her drink. Her face was puzzled. "He's in shock. He's doing all the right things and saying all the right things, but you feel he's on automatic. Completely mechanical. Of course, it's worse for him, in a way."

"Isabel means that Bradley is very fond of Scott— the Cushing boy."

"The boy the girls were talking to last night?"

"That's right. Lindsay and Angela had pizza at Sidonie's. Called out for it and then took a walk. It was a mild night," she added, as if she too had gone on autopilot.

"How far away is his house?"

"Not far. What would it be, Ken? About a hundred yards from here and maybe twice as much again on the other side to the Ursons?"

"I'd think so. The aim was to make a park-like setting."

Isabel waved this off impatiently. "Scott was playing with a golf club out in front of the house, and the girls stopped to talk to him."

The word *club* touched a nerve. "Clubbed to death" stuck in my mind, along with Angela saying, "I shouldn't have left her."

"Angela was tired and came home," Isabel continued, "so Scott was the last person to see Lindsay."

"I suppose any one of us could have been in that position," I said. "Or is there something about Scott that adds a sinister note?"

"I don't want to suggest anything," Isabel said, but her husband was less restrained.

"That kid's been nothing but trouble for years. I don't think he hurt Lindsay, I'm not saying that, but he's a handful. That's why Bradley's spent such a lot of time with him. He's been kind of a father figure to the boy. And to have this happen!"

"There was never anything serious," Isabel said quickly. "Broken windows. Uprooted plants. Nothing really serious."

"You took it seriously enough when he broke all the windows in our garage," said Ken. "People are going to wonder."

"No one's saying anything like that," Isabel corrected. "Everyone knows it was a transient. Someone up from the city or something."

"Wasn't it a bit late for golf by the time the girls stopped by?" I asked.

"He had the big outside lights on," Isabel said. "Everyone plays golf here. The yards are so big. And with those plastic practice balls there's really not much danger."

"You just never worried," Ken said. But it as clear to all of us that he wasn't talking about golf. "You just never worried about the people in Branch Hill."

I WOKE UP EARLY the next morning and sat by the window reading until I heard Ken's car. Although I believed that the Brownings were glad to have us around the house, I was pretty sure they weren't up for company. Isabel had gone back over to the Ursons' late—I'd heard the phone and her car—and as far as I knew, she hadn't come back. Angela went to school with her father. I was surprised to see that she was going, but Branch Hill seemed to have a passion for normalcy. The gallery had called almost indecently quickly to tell Harry that the opening was still on, and when I went down to the kitchen, Martha assured me that all the kids would be in school.

"Was Angela feeling better this morning?" I asked.

Martha's expression was subtly ambiguous. "Angela said the grief counselor would be there." I couldn't tell from her tone of voice what Angela's reaction to that would be.

"Grief counselor?"

"There are a lot of accidents in Branch Hill. Too many young people with fast cars. And too much liquor. They have a crash almost every spring around prom time. And sometimes with the winter parties. Angela knows," Martha continued, "that she's not to ride with just anyone. And never at night."

"Very sensible," I said, as Martha poured some orange juice for me. "Angela seemed very frightened yesterday."

"It's a frightening thing to find one of your friends has been murdered."

"Yes," I said, although Angela supposedly had not known the cause of death any more than I had. "She seems a sensitive child—with rather a delicate conscience."

Martha looked at me. "In what way?"

"She seemed to blame herself for not staying with Lindsay. For not walking home with her."

"It could have been her," Martha said. "She could have been the one who stopped to talk."

"I tried to tell her that, but I'm not great with children. Besides, I don't imagine danger ever crossed her mind. Not here, I mean."

"The world's in an awful mess," Martha said. "Would you like eggs?"

"No, thank you. This is just fine."

"Then I'll get to work. I didn't get much done yesterday."

As I ate my cereal and toast, I read about the killing in both the local paper and *The New York Times*. Lindsay Urson, age 14, a pupil at the Branch Hill Academy, had died from multiple blows to the back of her skull. Death was apparently all but instantaneous, and she had not been sexually assaulted, although there was a jagged shallow puncture wound below her left shoulder. She had been wearing a lavender cotton poncho over a long batik print dress and a pink T-shirt. I remembered the dress and the pink shirt, a shy expression, beautiful hair, potential grace. She had been last seen talking to her neighbor, Scott Cushing, also 14, who lived in the house nearest the Urson residence. Cushing claimed to have said good night around nine-twenty, when he brought in his golfing equipment and turned off the outside lights. This probably could not be substantiated, I thought, because his grandparents had been at the party and his mother had also been out.

The police apparently had not yet found anyone who had seen the girl after she left the Valons' yard for

home, and the time of death was therefore estimated
between nine-twenty-five and midnight. Lindsay Urson apparently had been killed where she was found,
no more than one hundred yards from her home. Only
chance, coincidence, and a damp morning had de-
layed the discovery until the Rosen boys raced down
the path in the grove and nearly fell over her body lying face down in the leaves.

I skimmed the rest of the paper, checked the interminable progress of the federal budget, the weather
forecast, and the comics, then pushed back my chair
and went out the front door. Ken had given us both
keys and, as Harry didn't have to be at the gallery until noon, I decided to go for a walk and let him sleep.

It was just eight-thirty, but the neighborhood already seemed deserted. The big, late-model cars that
had filled the driveways last night had already rolled
off to the city or to the many corporate and financial
headquarters on the outskirts of town. The children
had been driven to a variety of private schools leaving
an eerie tranquility. Somewhere an early-arriving lawn
crew started a mower. Otherwise, it was quiet, the im-
maculate lawns undisturbed, the perfectly pruned
bushes silent except for a few noisy jays and mock-
ingbirds. Here and there I noticed bicycles carelessly
left out, along with a few baseball bats, soccer balls,
and other sports paraphernalia. The Valons' yard
showed a skateboard and several tennis balls, and I
noticed that the ground to the right of the house was
badly chewed up from young Cushing's golf practice.
Otherwise, the compound was as tidy as a museum, a
very rich late-twentieth-century Sturbridge Village.

I saw the footpath that ran from behind the yellow plastic police lines into the miniature wood where Lindsay Urson had died. A few steps farther on I could see the green lawn at the other side. Sixty feet? Seventy? No longer than the typical suburban backyard. Lindsay Urson had, I supposed, been on her way home and, impatient with the serpentine track, had briefly left the brightly lit road for the grove. Beyond, she would have seen the lights of the far curve of the roadway and of her own house, and it could not have seemed dangerous in that mild and pleasant night to use the familiar track.

I wondered if she had heard footsteps, if she had turned. The news reports said "struck in the back of the head." Someone had been waiting—but who would that be, who knew the neighborhood habits well enough to predict where Lindsay would walk? Or else someone had seen the girl cross toward the trees and followed, striking before she had had time to register her danger.

I would have liked to examine the path, but a police van was parked on the grass, and I could see figures moving behind the trees, sifting the dirt and leaves for clues. A stolid-looking young officer stationed at the edge of the grove was pacing back and forth, smoking a cigarette. When he saw me on the walk he stopped, suspicious.

"Morning," I said. "Have you been here all night?"

"Just since six."

"The place seems pretty deserted now."

"This is strictly a bedroom town. We don't want the press marching through." He gave me another sharp look.

"I'm just visiting here," I said. I had one of my cards in my pocket and I handed it over. "Do you know if the security system people are around? I've recommended their firm to some of my clients, and I'm naturally interested to know if they had some sort of equipment failure."

The cop shrugged. "Far as I know they were always reliable. I haven't seen a truck come in, but they'd probably check the wall first."

"I'll walk over that way. Was the ground wet?" I asked, looking toward the path.

"Footprints of half the kids in the compound and all the dogs," he said.

"With their adult owners, too, no doubt."

"That's about it."

"A terrible thing," I said.

"Yeah. There'll be a lot of heat until we get him. You know, every car going out this morning stopped to ask what I was doing and was there anything new."

"They didn't think it could happen here."

"That's right. But being in the business of security, you know better. Right?"

"Yes."

"It can happen anywhere," he said. "Any time." With this cheerful credo, he lit another cigarette and resumed his pacing.

I skirted the police lines and walked around the trees. The yellow plastic tapes cut off almost all of the grove, but at the far side, I was able to look at the path. It was hard, trampled dirt, half covered with old leaves. I could see other little, less traveled tracks—the Indian trails and secret passages of childhood, with hiding places and ambushes behind each tree. The main path crossed the grass and rejoined the sidewalk, but it would have been possible, I saw now, for someone to make his way through the trees and into the shadows of some of the big rhododendrons and azaleas that dotted the lawns. From the security point of view, the famous park-like setting had not been the wisest choice.

The emissary of Total Protection Corporation had the same reaction. He was a neat, wiry fellow with wavy black hair and rosy cheeks that made him look like an oversized schoolboy. I found him stamping around the perimeter of the Estates with two technicians, laboriously checking each of the sensors along the top of the wall and getting more exasperated every minute.

"Perfect," he said to me after I'd introduced myself and he'd recognized my name. "Every single one in perfect order."

"And the reception equipment?"

"Ditto. Brand new. This is my biggest contract. Am I going to short them on equipment? Don't be ridiculous. I told the police that yesterday when I checked."

"This is the second time around?"

"Yes. Oh, yes! We worked 'til—when was it, Joey? Ten?"

"Ten-thirty at least," said Joey, a thin man with a buckskin-colored complexion. "I wasn't home 'til eleven."

"The circuits are fine. Anybody went over this wall, there'd have been a blip on the screen, a buzzer in the guard's booth—and, get this, a record on the computer. Nothing. They says to me, they says check it again. I'm checking it again. But am I going to find anything?"

"Was Davis on duty?"

"My best man. He's been with the company ten years. He was the first one hired—him and Joey here. Never a complaint. Absolutely reliable."

"And the computer backs him up?"

"You got it. All the evidence says inside job. No exit, either."

"Unless someone drove or walked out past the gate house."

"Right. And Davis checks every plate number. He's sure no stranger came in or out."

"I can believe that. He insisted we give our rental car number and came out and checked the plate to make sure it matched."

"See? Just what I'm saying."

"But not a popular discovery."

"You bet. Not an *acceptable* discovery. But they'll have to face it. Unless we come up with a malfunction, the poor kid was killed by one of her neighbors."

FOUR

THE GALLERY WAS JAMMED. Now and then as the sea of champagne- and sherry-toting art lovers parted, I caught a glimpse of the prints hanging on the far side of the room and of Harry holding court in front of the brilliantly hued advertising posters displayed in the center. Then there would be another spate of arrivals to be welcomed and a trickle of departing guests to be thanked. I was pleased to see that many of the latter left carrying mailing tubes with the exhibition poster, and that there was a constant stream of buyers in and out of Georgie Cole's office. In fact, she'd been so busy that I'd been installed near the door as official greeter.

"Oh, isn't this marvelous!" a well-dressed woman with a severely geometric haircut exclaimed.

"A wonderful turnout," I agreed.

"A super show. And just what we needed at the moment."

I agreed to that, too, and she didn't need to say more. The tension in the Estates had left everyone frazzled, and even in Branch Hill proper, the initial sense of disbelief was gradually sliding into suspicion. There had already been neighborhood meetings with the police, the Council, and the unfortunate manager of Total Protection Corporation, and more were planned. Meanwhile, police cars cruised in and out of the Estates all day, and the search for clues and weapons moved from the grove to the manicured shrubbery beyond with a gentle amoeba-like motion that would inevitably reach the fine houses along the drive.

Of course, we'd all been interviewed by the police. Harry and I could add little, beyond confirming that the girls had been in the house around seven and that there had been a late-night call at the Brownings'. Angela had demanded Martha's presence when her turn came—I heard the discussion of that point on my way upstairs. Ken had missed the detectives the first time through, and the second as well. The undiscouraged detectives returned at six-fifteen in the morning and interviewed him at breakfast. Later, Ken nervously kept bringing up the subject of the interviews, professing such amazement that his family had been troubled that I'd begun to wonder if he had something to hide. This afternoon, in fact, I'd returned to see a squad car pulling out of the drive: The Branch Hill police were certainly thorough.

That had become one of the talking points. Everybody in the Estates seemed impelled to relate their own brief moment of suspicion and vindication. The officers had arrived for one at dinner, had caught another in the shower, and a third, still in pajamas. Some of the Brownings' neighbors found this annoying, some, absurd; underneath were other emotions. Isabel made a point of telling me they'd have to keep all the doors locked, and Martha now waited at the door every afternoon when Angela's bus was due. Twice I heard her tell the girl that she couldn't go out alone, and in the afternoon the broad lawns blossomed with baby-sitters, nannies, au pairs, housekeepers, even the young mothers themselves still in their tennis dresses. They watched their neighbors with cool, speculative eyes, as if thinking not just "Which of us?", but "Which of us can we bear to suspect?"

And while they watched, their conversations slid from the officers' visits to the delays in finding the killer, to oblique speculation. As I handed out the gallery's leaflets and touted the expensive full-color catalog, I heard the familiar phrases and the fear under the deliberately brittle and sophisticated chat. Sometimes I heard Scott Cushing's name and sometimes "poor Sidonie" or "poor Angela," and once "poor Alex Valon." Amen to that. According to Georgie Cole, who despite her meek airs seemed uncommonly well informed, the Cushing boy was a bad apple.

"Not entirely his fault," she'd told me while we opened the printer's boxes full of leaflets. "The mother is something."

"No dad?"

"Fortunately. I heard he beat her—the boy, too. That was the story when she arrived here. I think it's one reason the Valons agreed to move in. Dottie's so nice, don't you think?"

"To protect them, you mean? To discourage the son-in-law?"

"The ex-son-in-law, yes. Though once you know Cynthia—" She left the thought hanging.

"Not the best background for the boy."

"No. He's been hostile since he was a little kid. He went after one of our cats with an air rifle. He and the Sloan boy from our street. I called his mother, and I must say that I never saw him around our place again."

"I've heard Bradley Urson spent a lot of time with him."

Georgie raised her eyebrows. "He's Bradley's project. His latest project. The most recent of a string of unfortunates."

"And what kind of luck does he have with them?"

"Oh, you know. They're around for a while. Bradley gets them part-time jobs. Eventually they go off."

"Scott Cushing sounds a bit too young for that plan."

"Well, Scott's a neighbor. The others are imports—like William. Haven't you seen William Brighton?"

I was puzzled and shook my head.

"William with the hair. Very Dürer-self-portrait. Tall, blond—quite angelic looking despite the mustache and bare feet."

"He doesn't sound like Branch Hill at all."

"You'd be surprised. Actually this one's from Greenwich. Intelligent, but very troubled and disconnected. He was an art major and actually has some talent. I'm sure you'll see him at the opening."

"And where does William live?"

"At the Gores' house. Bradley arranged that. He felt William needed a stable family environment. William drives the kids back and forth to school, washes the cars—odd jobs. The thing is," Georgie said, lowering her voice, "he's inclined to roam about at all hours. No one seems to know where he goes or what he does, except that he always has his camera."

"Unfortunate habit."

"Yes, indeed," Georgie agreed.

As it happened, William did turn up at the opening, a tall, shambling boy with a vague, sulky expression who stood silently in front of each print in turn, then joined the group around Harry. I noticed that beyond a few vague gestures of greeting, the other teenagers rather avoided him, but I was soon distracted by new arrivals and by questions about the catalog. The macabre sensation of the murder was quite out of my mind when Alex Valon appeared.

"Anna, could I see you privately for a minute?" His voice was soft, barely above a whisper, but something in his tone assured me that the matter was urgent.

"Oh, Alex. How good of you to come." I smiled at a woman who was collecting more than her share of leaflets and asked one of the volunteers to take my place. "Maybe the back? I think even the front porch is occupied."

"A nice turnout," Alex said as we made our way down the hall. "Poor Sidonie Urson would have been pleased."

"Yes. Harry and I felt awkward about going on with the opening, but nobody wanted to cancel."

"The tyranny of arrangements," Alex said with a sigh.

"I'm afraid I can't stay away too long," I said, as I opened the door onto the little back porch.

"This will be brief," Alex said. "I need your help for Scott."

"You'd better tell me how and what's wrong."

"The police have found the murder weapon."

"That's since—"

"This afternoon. All unofficial yet, but I don't think there's much doubt. They came to our house first because they knew that Scott had been out playing with the clubs that night. I recognized one of my old drivers."

"Are you're absolutely sure?"

"Without a doubt. It's an old-fashioned club. I let Scott have an old set to practice with. I doubt there's another one like it anywhere around."

"Where did they find the club? Did they tell you that?"

"Yes, but not then. I know the police chief well—we're on a number of committees together. Apparently the pieces had been thrown into some bushes. I don't know whose property."

"The pieces?"

"The shaft had been broken in half."

"And were the ends sharp? The broken ends?"

"Well, splintery."

I was thinking of that odd puncture wound. Lindsay had been struck repeatedly from behind. Then the club had broken, and the enraged assailant had stabbed his victim—once. That seemed odd to me.

"Have the police questioned Scott yet?"

"No. They plan to see him tomorrow. When our lawyer is present."

"There may be fingerprints. If he was playing with the club, his will surely be on it."

"I know. That's one of the troubling things."

"Something else troubles me. The press reports said that Scott picked up his golf equipment and went inside around nine-twenty. How likely was that? Was he a tidy child?"

"Not excessively, certainly. His room is reasonable, but he is inclined to be careless with possessions. Too easily come by, if you ask me, but I'm not raising the boy."

"When I walked by your house the morning after the killing, I noticed some toys—a skateboard, I forget what else—in front of the house. Was that typical?"

"I'm afraid so."

"Yet Scott told the police he brought his golfing equipment inside?"

"Yes, I was there when he talked to them."

"I see. But it is at least possible he forgot a club? The yard, even well lighted, must have shadows, places where one might overlook a club."

"It's possible."

"I'd suggest that to your lawyer. And I'd check the yard at night—with the lights. Find out exactly where he was practicing."

"Yes," said Alex, nodding. "Yes, that's a good idea, too, Anna. Thank you." He seemed grateful for even those poor scraps of advice, and I could see how much this normally confident man needed direction, orders, a plan. Disaster does that to you; after Harry's heart attack, I knew the feeling.

"Look, I don't know the boy, but it seems to me to have been an impulsive crime. A sudden, violent impulse with whatever was at hand—in this case a golf club. Possibly one left lying on the grass."

"That's what I believe. Scott is a difficult boy, but not vicious."

"I suspect it's in his favor that he mentioned bringing in the clubs."

Alex nodded. "He could have said he thought he left one or two out, couldn't he?"

"Yes." But I was thinking that there were so many possibilities. So much depends on intelligence, on foresight, on personality.

"I want to do all I can," Alex was saying. "I want you to be involved."

"Alex, I'd like to help, but I have to get back to Washington. We're only going to stay until the service for Lindsay. We felt we owed that to her family, but—"

"You misunderstand. I want to employ your services. At your normal rates, of course."

"Your police department here seems very competent. If you have a good lawyer, and I'm sure you do, he'll be able to suggest someone local who's reliable. Someone who knows the area has all the advantages in this sort of case."

"You're staying at the Brownings'. You're an old friend of mine. That will be enough to open doors. And I can arrange for police cooperation."

"I'll have to think about it, Alex. You know that if I start looking into the case, there's no certainty about what I'll find—or if it will help Scott. I'm not like a lawyer. All the cards are going to be on the table."

Alex gave a wan smile. "As I recall, you had no hesitation about that in your last case for Independence Mutual."

"No, and that's why it was my last investigation for them. I like you. I'd just as soon we stay friends."

He put both hands on the rail of the porch and leaned over it with a sour expression. For all his diffident charm, Alex is from the privileged class, used to getting his own way. "I want to know," he said. "Scott's my grandson. My only grandson." He paused, looked down at his immaculately polished shoes for a moment, then turned to me. "I believe he's innocent. I believe that strongly enough to want to know for sure."

"All right. What about this: We'll be here until after the service. I'll see Harry home and return if necessary—and if I'm making progress. Fair enough?"

"I'd appreciate that, Anna," he said, shaking my hand. "I'd really appreciate that."

"I'll talk to you tomorrow. And I'd like to talk to Scott after he's seen the police."

"Yes," Alex said. "Fine." He glanced at his watch. "I'm not coming back in. I haven't told Dottie yet about the club, and I don't want her to hear it on the news."

I said good-bye and watched him walk down the rows of expensive vehicles to his car. To tell the truth, I'd have preferred to stay clear of the whole mess. But if the police had the weapon, they might have prints—with luck, prints other than Scott Cushing's. In that happy eventuality, I might not have to be involved. I consoled myself further with the thought that Alex was probably over-reacting and returned to the gallery. The festivities were beginning to wind down; the crowd had thinned to the serious art lovers and the late arrivals, and I was able to ignore the book table and check on Harry.

"Fine, fine," he said to my whispered inquiry. He held up his glass of fruit punch. "Not a drop of champagne, either."

"Good boy. Your doctor would be pleased."

"Doctors don't know everything," he said airily. "This has been fun, in spite of everything."

"Everyone's been very impressed."

He smiled and turned to thank some visitors for coming. I heard him say, "Yes, we can ship right away. Mrs. Cole has arranged to fax the orders directly to my workshop," when there was an angry voice, then a thump and the unmistakable sound of breaking china and glass. Someone had been pushed— or had stumbled—onto the refreshments table, which tilted, sending the punch bowl skidding onto the floor along with a tray of empty champagne glasses, half-empty platters of canapés, and several bottles. An angry-looking boy with short black hair picked himself up off the floor and shook cheese dip and bits of cracker and shrimp from his jacket. Georgie Cole scurried over with a handful of napkins and began mopping the back of the coat, while tall, pale William watched her expressionlessly, his large hands picking at the ends of his frayed shirt. I guessed something had been said—perhaps about the killing, perhaps about his nocturnal rambles.

"I don't like the look of this," Harry said. He walked quickly across to the table. "Needs more of the yellow stuff," he said to the boy with the damaged jacket. "Can't hang it as is. I think we'd better have Mrs. Cole send it to the cleaners at our expense. Good enough?"

"He shoved me," the boy said, still angry.

"What's an opening without some controversy?" Harry said. "Go with Mrs. Cole and give her your name and phone. You'll take care of the coat?" he asked her.

"Yes, and I'll call Norman to get the mop. Nothing serious," she said briskly.

As I helped one of the volunteers right the table, I saw my husband put his hand on William's arm and steer him toward the door. "Damn gallery champagne," he remarked as they went by. "It's always stronger than you think, isn't it?"

The boy didn't answer, but he went out meekly. I saw that Georgie Cole was right: His features were exceptionally good, though his expression was oddly lacking in emotion. He reminded me of Botticelli's wayward, tarnished *La Primavera* and gave a strong impression of damage, of unhealed wounds and unresolved troubles. Later, I asked my husband if my initial guess about the little fracas had been correct.

"Well, that's what Georgie said, anyway. I didn't get anything out of William. Apparently, the kid with the jacket—Tucker something, Hayes, I think—is a bit of a loudmouth. He said he just asked William where he was Sunday night. Georgie says he probably asked half a dozen times—that's the sort he is."

"Sounds about right."

"The other kid's a funny one. He knows a lot about art. We had quite a talk earlier about Rauschenberg, and he was very articulate. But I couldn't get any coherent account of what had happened with the table. Though he said he was sorry."

"I imagine he's under a bit of stress," I said. "If I interpret correctly what Georgie said earlier, he's the neighborhood's first choice as perpetrator."

FIVE

WHEN WE GOT BACK from the gallery after supper in downtown Branch Hill, Ken met us at the door to ask how the opening had gone.

"Really well," I said.

"And very well arranged and run," Harry added.

"I'm glad to hear that. It'll be good for Sidonie and Bradley to hear that, too."

"How are they doing?"

Ken shrugged. "Isabel has hardly been home, but she said Caroline, the other daughter, had gotten in. That has to help."

He stood by the stairs as if he wanted to talk, so I said, "I think Harry should go up and rest. Doctor's orders."

"Oh, of course. I'd forgotten you've been out all day. Maybe Anna could spare me a minute?"

"Sure."

"I want to give Angela a poster," Harry said. "Is she with Martha?"

"No, upstairs in her room, I think. Martha won't be back from canasta yet. She and the Valons' cook and a couple of the other housekeepers play once a week."

"I'll drop this off to Angela," Harry said.

"I'll be up in a few minutes," I told him and followed Ken into the living room.

"Would you like a drink? I always have Scotch and soda at night."

"No, no thanks. I had some of that gallery champagne."

I sat down in one of the comfortable upholstered chairs, while Ken fiddled with his drink, adding more ice and more Scotch.

"I wanted to ask what you thought about the investigation. Being in the business, so to speak."

"Well, my line of work is a bit different—fraud cases, usually. Though not exclusively."

"Nonetheless."

"As far as I can see, they're doing a pretty good job. They seem thorough, pretty tactful, persistent."

"They've had over a hundred people employed."

"It's a big case. There's a lot to check. How many homes are in the Estates? Thirty or so?"

Ken nodded.

"That's just the permanent residents. If there was a visitor no one knows about, if some outsider did get in . . . Do you see what I'm saying?"

"But surely they could eliminate some people right away?"

"Children under three, grannies of eighty—sure. That still leaves the rest of us. How are they to know? They have to find out where each of us was at the proper time. That eliminates another group. And so on. It can be very slow."

Ken looked uncomfortable.

"And there's no guarantee they'll find the killer. Not even if he—or she—is one of your neighbors."

"They say there's a lot of information."

"But it may not be the crucial information that enables separation of the innocent from the guilty. For one thing, if it was done on impulse—well, there may not be a clear motive."

"So we're all under suspicion in the meantime." I was surprised at the bitterness in his voice.

"Well—yes, more or less."

Ken had been perched on the edge of the soft leather couch. Now he jumped up and went to stand in front of the fireplace. A cinder had come out onto the hearth, and he moved it back and forth with the toe of his shoe, leaving a black smear on the bricks. "I may have done something foolish," he said.

I was tempted to say, "Who hasn't," but I kept quiet.

"I told a small lie to the police."

"The police don't regard too many lies as small."

"I thought—I thought it was such a terrible thing that they'd get it solved, that someone would confess, that something—incriminating—would be found right away."

"The smoking gun?"

"Yeah. I couldn't believe it at first," he said, sitting down on the couch and leaning forward with his elbows on his knees. There was an intimate touch to Ken's conversation that I hadn't noticed before. "I kept thinking—it could have been Angela. You don't have children?"

I shook my head.

"You don't know the feeling, then. The feeling of absolute vulnerability. The feeling that they're out there and you can't protect them."

"With anyone you love, you get that feeling."

"More strongly with children," he said. "Much more strongly with children."

I didn't argue. And there was a brief silence. The hypnotic flickering of the fire was soothing, and I noticed how Ken's eyes kept moving back toward the flames.

"I just figured it would be all cleared up," he said.

"So you felt what the police didn't have to know couldn't matter?"

"Something like that."

"But they feel differently?"

"I'm beginning to feel like a suspect. Listen, dinner was over the other night when—around ten?"

"That's about right. Harry and I went upstairs around eleven."

"Yes. You went up early. Bradley and Sidonie and Isabel and I had another drink. Alex and Dottie left when you went upstairs. We were all together all evening. You'd think that was good enough."

"From the police point of view, it all depends on time of death. You know those times are a bit elastic."

"Isabel and I went upstairs. That was midnight. She went right to bed. I—I took a shower. She was asleep when I got out of the bathroom. I got dressed again and went for a drive."

"Out of the Estates?"

"Yeah. Straight out. I didn't see anything. Had I seen anything, noticed anything, I'd have mentioned it to the police. You can be sure of that."

"What time did you get back?"

"You didn't ask where I went," he said.

"You'll tell me if you want to," I said. "It may not be relevant—unless you're someone's alibi. Then it's important."

He gave a little half smile. "I got back at two A.M. I was lucky—I thought. I'd just gotten into bed when the phone started ringing. I let Isabel answer it. I let it wake her up and pretended to be half asleep."

"The gateman must have a record."

"Sometimes Davis can turn a blind eye," Ken said.

"Then how did the police find out?"

"I'm not sure they have," he said. "But they're suspicious."

"They're trained to be suspicious. That's why it's better to be candid with them."

"I didn't want Isabel to know, that's all. Things have been going pretty well with us lately. Just sometimes—"

I didn't want to hear his confession. "If you're asking me, I think you should tell the police. They will ask where you went, of course. But otherwise, they'll keep after you—wasting their time and maybe turning up things you'd rather they didn't. And in this sort of community—"

"You don't need to remind me of that," he said abruptly. "Are you sure you won't have a drink, Anna? I hate drinking alone."

"No, but thanks. I should really make sure Harry has taken all his medicine."

"We all have our little weaknesses," Ken said almost angrily. "Women don't always understand that."

"Murder is more than a little weakness," I said. "Consider the alternatives."

"They shouldn't be bothering us in the first place," he said, and I decided that the drink in his hand was by no means his first.

"They're just doing their job," I said. I had the feeling Ken could become an uncomfortable conversationalist. I said good night and went upstairs, wondering what he'd left out and how good Davis's memory might be.

Upstairs, Harry was sitting in bed watching the Mets.

"How's the game?"

"Mets by five. Would you switch over to the Yankees?"

"Where's your remote? I thought there was one with this set."

"I don't know," he said, but when I got out of the bathtub, he remembered that he'd pocketed it by mistake. "I think I left it down on the hall table. It was when we were getting ready to go out."

"I'll get it for you," I said, picking up his bathrobe.

"I don't need it."

"But they'll wonder where it's disappeared to. It's no bother. Unless I see Ken again."

"A confiding mood?"

"Sort of. He was out on the night of the murder between twelve and two A.M. A bit late to make him a suspect, but the thing is, he didn't tell the police."

"A lady friend somewhere," Harry suggested. "He's a restless one."

"What do you mean?"

"The other night at dinner, he was up and down like a jack-in-the-box."

"That's right. Very much the helpful husband."

"And he was out, too. I went into the kitchen at one point to get a glass of water for my pills. He was just coming in the back door. Taking out the garbage, he said."

"That's something you should have told the police."

Harry shrugged. "He wasn't gone long enough to get into trouble."

"Probably not. But this whole thing could be awkward since Alex has asked me to look around and see what I can do."

"And will you?"

"For a day or so, nothing more. I'll get that remote control," I said and left without bothering to put on my slippers. A discussion of schedules was to be avoided. I didn't want to leave Harry at this stage of his convalescence, and I didn't want to discover he'd just as soon have a few days free of quasi-medical surveillance.

The Brownings' upper hall was on some sort of automatic dimmer, and although neither it nor the foyer downstairs was particularly well lit, I found the remote-control without much trouble. I had just started toward the stairs when I heard the door to the kitchen open. I turned to see Angela. She froze half through the doorway, her face rigid with terror, and as I started to greet her, she gave a muffled shriek and put her hand over her mouth.

"What's wrong?" I said. "It's Anna. Harry left the remote for the upstairs TV on the hall table."

She nodded, and I could see the recognition in her eyes. "Oh, you frightened me!"

"I'm sorry. No slippers, no noise. I'm sure you've been jumpy. I didn't know you were downstairs."

"I always say good night to Martha."

I saw that she was shaking, and I went over and took her arm. "Sit down for a minute. Do you want me to get Martha?"

"No, Martha's gone to bed. I'm okay. I've just been so nervous since—"

"It's the aftershock."

"Like an earthquake," she said with a touch of her pert intelligence.

"Sort of. I've had the same thing happen. You're fine in a crisis and then afterwards, boom—it all hits you."

She nodded.

"And you went right back to school. That must have been a strain."

"Mom wanted me to talk to Mr. Gibbons—he's the grief counselor. And all my friends were there. Martha hasn't wanted me to be out at night at all and otherwise—"

"Martha is understandably worried. But you'd told me Lindsay was an acquaintance, a neighbor, not a special friend. Is that right?"

"Yes," she said with some spirit. "Because we were together just before—everyone makes out that we were best friends. Everyone's so sorry for me. 'How awful for you'—you know the way."

"And that bothers you?"

She nodded.

"Who were Lindsay's special friends?"

Angela shrugged. "She wasn't that popular. The gymnastics crowd mostly."

"This was at school?"

"No. At Sue Tansi's. It's a private gymnastics school. That's where Lindsay spent most of her time.

It was just coincidence that I saw her that afternoon and we said we'd have a pizza because our folks were going to the party for you guys."

"And do you know anything else about her?"

"You're not the police," Angela said. "The police asked me these questions."

"I thought you might want to talk about her, that's all. Sometimes people don't really want to talk to the police."

Angela shrugged.

"Not about awkward things," I went on. "Like whether or not Lindsay was involved with something she shouldn't have been. Drugs, maybe. Or an older boyfriend?"

Angela jumped up. "I'm tired. I have to go to bed now," she said. Her dark clothes accentuated her pallor, and with that and her nervousness and her thick hair pulled back from her broad, white forehead, she looked like an unlucky Tudor princess set for the ax.

"Good night. I'm sorry I frightened you."

"It was nothing," Angela said quickly. "It's just everyone's afraid of strangers now."

"You're sure you don't want me to get Martha?"

"No. 'Night, Anna." Angela was up the stairs and down the hall like a sprinter.

I went back across the hall to the kitchen wing, but everything was dark except for a single light over the stove. Martha had disappeared for the night. Isabel was still at the Ursons', and Ken was drinking in the living room. I had the feeling that Angela had not gone in to say good night to him. An odd household. An odd neighborhood. I remembered the conversations at the dinner party the first night: the concern with safety, the desire for a secure neighborhood. What had Ken said? For a place where children could play out at night. In the half-dark kitchen, the big windows reflected the blackness outside. The clock ticked; otherwise, not a sound. On one wall, a tiny red sensor light glowed. Everything had been done to ensure safety, but the house didn't feel secure, and certainly Angela hadn't felt safe when she'd seen me standing in the hall. As I went back to our room, I thought I'd like to know how she and Lindsay Urson had spent their unsupervised time.

"I told you not to bother," Harry said when I opened the door. "I'm just going to sleep."

"What?"

"The remote. Wasn't that what you were looking for?"

"Oh." I fished in my pocket for the control and set it on the TV. Then I sat down on the edge of his bed. "Did you give Angela the poster?"

"Yes. Autographed it for her, too. It's on her bulletin board."

"Was she in her room, or did you see her in the hall?"

"What is this, Anna? I knocked on her door and she said 'Come in'."

"Was she surprised to see you?"

"Not at all. She was full of chat. Said the school art class was going to see the show next week. What's the matter?"

"I don't know. I was in the hall when she came out of the kitchen and she was so frightened when she saw me that I thought she'd faint."

"Trick of the light, maybe."

"She said she'd been jumpy and nervous with everyone."

"She did ask who was there. That's right. She did ask that."

"But she sounded okay?"

"Sure. Gave me all the neighborhood gossip—Tucker Hayes is an asshole of the first order, and the police have been hassling William Brighton."

"And Lindsay. Did she say anything about Lindsay Urson?"

"No, except that the Madrigal Society was going to sing at her funeral."

SIX

THE SERVICE WAS at St. George's, the local Episcopal church, a brownstone Gothic with lots of stained glass and carved woodwork. The altar was surrounded by wreaths from the neighbors, the gallery, Bradley's firm, the gymnastics center, and Lindsay's day-school class. Large numbers of her classmates had turned out for the service, bussed in from their campus north of town. They hung around the back of the church for a time, uncertain of proper funeral etiquette, until one of their instructors took them in hand and ushered them to a block of seats toward the front. Among the other mourners I recognized some of the Brownings' neighbors, the women in smart low pumps and dark dresses, the men in sober pinstripes like a phalanx of bankers. The organist pumped out an interminable and lugubrious prelude, and everyone felt not just sad, but acutely awkward: The deaths of children leave us unprepared. The usual clichés of condolence are unsuitable and fate seems not just malign, but unseemly.

Right at eleven, the rose-covered casket was rolled in from the back. The family followed: Sidonie and Caroline Urson wore black veils; Bradley's face was puffy and pale, his eyes expressionless. They walked slowly and heavily down the aisle and sat in the front pew. A few soft chords sounded in the choir loft, and the singers began the *Kyrie* from a Monteverdi mass.

The voices were pure and strong, particularly the lead soprano, whom I realized must be Angela. The voice was remarkable, without a tremor despite the emotional circumstances. Several of her classmates were weeping, but her clear soprano soared over the lower tones of the choir, seamless, tender, and sweet.

When the music ended, the principal of the day school stepped up and said the expected things. Then the proprietress of the gymnastics school described the deceased's gymnastic abilities, and one plump, nervous girl bid Lindsay farewell from her classmates before the minister read the burial service—the old, unimproved rendition, which starts, "I am the resurrection and the life…" The choir sang a Mozart *Agnus Dei*, and, after a final prayer, the sad procession returned through the church, followed by the rest of the congregation. The sleek funeral home limos and the hearse were already lined up at the curb when we came out murmuring our regrets. Sidonie's eyes flickered under her veil.

"How kind of you to stay for the service," she said as I touched her hand.

"It was the least we could do. We're so very sorry."

"Please come and see me before you leave," she said. Then she shook the next hand in line. "Thank you for coming. It was very kind."

Harry and I went down the steps and stood with the other mourners, waiting for the Ursons to leave for the cemetery. The Valons were there, looking awkward and heartsick, as well as several people we'd met at the opening. We lingered, talking to them and to some others who recognized Harry from the publicity photos but who hadn't yet seen the show, and we were still there when the choir emerged. Angela was talking intently to a tall blond man who, Dottie Valon whispered, was the choir director. Just behind them walked a dark-haired woman in a severe black dress and gloves.

"Wonderful music," I said to them. "I'm just sorry we didn't hear you on a happier occasion."

"This is Peter," Angela said, putting her arm through his. "Peter Laurimer. Our director and teacher."

He had a youthful face, with mild blue eyes and a soft, tentative mouth. After he shook our hands, he began introducing the others. The handsome dark-haired woman was Miriam Greene, the principal alto, and the tall, balding man, the bass, Lyle Briggs.

We introduced ourselves in turn and shook hands with them and with the other members of the group who were straggling out of the church.

"That Monteverdi piece is beautiful," Harry said.

"And so suitable, don't you think?" Miriam Greene asked. "We'd had some discussion about that."

"What could be suitable under the circumstances?" Peter asked with a touch of asperity. "It's just what's less unsuitable."

"Beautiful, though," I said. "I'm sure the family appreciated it."

"Oh, I'm sure," Miriam said, putting one of her black-gloved hands to her throat. "That's what I told Peter." With a sly smile, she moved closer to him and took his free arm. "The marvelous thing about Peter is that he's always very open to suggestions."

"Only if they're good ones," Angela said promptly, and I got the feeling that there was little love lost between the soprano and the alto.

"My suggestions are always good," Miriam said in a lordly tone, while Peter Laurimer looked uncomfortably like a felon apprehended by the woman on either side.

"And you specialize strictly in early music?" Harry asked. My husband is one of the peacemakers of the earth, impelled to nip uncomfortable scenes in the bud. Although this has ensured our domestic tranquility, it is not always conducive to discovery.

"Yes, pretty much so. A few ventures into Mozart, no later."

"Peter's favorite is Monteverdi," Angela said. "The greatest musician of all."

"Angela has crushes," Miriam said dismissively. "Look, they're ready to leave. I really think we ought to go to the cemetery."

"No, that's just for the family," said Angela.

"And close neighbors, too, surely."

"Mom said Mrs. Urson made it very clear: just family."

"I'm not sure," Peter began.

"It would look funny if some representatives of the Society didn't go," Miriam interrupted. "After singing." She set her face in a way that suggested vast resources of confidence and stubbornness. Angela was ready for an argument, but I noticed Peter shake his head very slightly.

"Naturally, Angela shouldn't go—the strain after all that's happened," Miriam said. "But we adults ought to make at least a token showing. Come on,

Peter, we'd better go. We'll see you at practice, Angela. Good-bye all.''

With another glance at the girl, Laurimer allowed himself to be led away. Angela hesitated, but one of the other teenagers called her, and she went off toward their school bus. Miriam Greene turned her head, then leaned over and whispered something to the choir director.

"There's the lute player," my husband remarked as we passed a thin gray-haired woman carrying an instrument case. "We wondered—it didn't sound quite like a guitar or anything else modern."

"We weren't sure how well the sound would carry," she said.

"It was very nice," I said. "We were telling the others we wished we could have heard the group on a happier occasion."

"We have a lot of concerts," she said, a smile lightening her angular face. "I'm Esther Reed. I didn't get to your opening, but Georgie Cole let me peek in the day before. It was very impressive."

Harry thanked her, and we exchanged small talk for a few minutes before she said, "Did you meet the others? I was supposed to get a ride back with Miriam. Mrs. Green, our alto."

"I think she decided someone should go along to the cemetery. She and Mr. Laurimer were going."

"The cemetery was to be private." I could see Esther Reed was irritated.

"That point was raised," Harry said dryly.

"But not carried? I'm not surprised. Once Miriam's mind is set—"

"Do you live in Branch Hill?" I asked. "We could give you a ride."

"Oh, I don't want to bother you. I would just walk if it weren't for the lute."

"Nonsense," Harry said. "After such beautiful music, we'd be pleased."

"Well, that's kind. It's not far. You'll turn left at the light when you leave the parking lot. Then it's the third right. Wharf Street."

Wharf Street ran down from the business center through an area of older homes, some of which had been converted to lawyers' and doctors' offices, then wound around a stretch of undeveloped salt marsh. It was a couple of miles to Esther Reed's house, and on the way we talked about the Madrigal Society. It was relatively new, despite its local eminence, and had been the inspiration of Peter Laurimer, who had arrived to be music instructor at the public school just five years before. Since the school job was part time, he made ends meet with private lessons and with the modest stipend raised by the Madrigal Society's concerts. "Well, not quite so modest any more," Esther corrected herself. "The concerts do surprisingly well."

"The music is very good," I said.

"Yes, Peter has peculiar talents."

"Peculiar?"

"He's a good musician, an ordinary good musician, if you know what I mean—he plays the piano well, the harpsichord even better, and he has a pleasant voice. What's peculiar, or I should say, unusual, is his feeling for early music. He seems to have a complete understanding of it. The rest of us look at the score and it's a nice tune, words on the page. I don't know if I'm expressing myself clearly, but Peter has a seventeenth-century soul.''

"I'm not sure that would be convenient," Harry said, turning around to look at Esther.

"I'm not sure it's convenient for Peter. Or for his family."

"He has a family?" I asked. The open flirtatiousness of some of the choir members had suggested other possibilities.

"He and Jill have three children. Two small girls and the baby. A little boy, I think. The next street's the one," she added. "It's hard to read the sign the way that hedge has grown."

Esther lived in a pretty gray shingled cape with flourishing beds of asters and chrysanthemums in front.

"Now that's what I call a garden," Harry said. "I wish I had my sketchbook with me."

"Thank you. I love it here along the water. Of course, Branch Hill isn't what it used to be. It was more like this once—unpretentious, a bit shabby, even, a beach place—but nice. This awful business with the Urson girl shows how we've changed."

"You don't subscribe to the 'outsider' theory, then?" I asked.

"That is the popular one," she replied, without answering my question. She took her lute from Harry with a smile, and after thanking us again, disappeared into her pretty house.

An interesting woman, I thought as we left her drive. And an observer. It was too bad she didn't live closer to the Estates.

WE ATE LUNCH at yet another of the town's bright
and trendy restaurants before returning to the Brownings'. Harry was to rest and pack, then visit the Ursons to thank Sidonie and to give her the guest book
from the opening. Armed with the hope that the fo-
rensic technicians would soon have prints from the
club, I set off for an interview with Master Scott
Cushing. His grandfather met me at the door, looking tired and worn down.

"Come in, come in. Scott's in the den."

"Have you heard anything more from the police?"

"No, not a word."

As I stepped inside, I noticed an old-fashioned ce-
ramic receptacle by the door. I noticed several leather-
wrapped handgrips in addition to the canes and um-
brellas. "Your clubs?"

"Yes," he said, drawing one out to show me. "I left
these in the hall for Scott to fool around with."

"Is your door ever left unlocked?"

"It's open all day when the weather's warm. Sometimes we hook the screen door." He gave a little
crooked smile. "Not the best security."

"I'm with you, Alex. You can have too much of a
good thing. Still—"

He nodded, no doubt thinking as I did that anyone
who knew the neighborhood might have known the
clubs were there and how to reach them.

"Through here," Alex said, opening a fine oak
door. "This is Scott."

A fair, solid-looking kid turned away from his Nin-
tendo game and gave me the once-over. "This is Anna
Peters," his grandfather said.

"Yeah. Hi."

"Turn that off," Alex said, "and come sit over here."

"Aw. I was at the fourth level," he said, but he switched off the device and the set. When he stood up, I saw he was nearly as tall as I am. I'd hoped for a little fellow; Scott could easily have passed for sixteen or seventeen.

"I want to ask you some questions about Sunday night," I said. "They're probably the same questions the police asked you, but I'd appreciate your going through everything again. All right?"

"Sure. It's your time," he said so indifferently that I added, "And maybe your future," before I caught myself. I'm not good with children.

He started fidgeting then, but began his account. His narration was more childish than his appearance, and it was clear that he was torn between the fear and horror of his position and a delight in being so much the center of attention.

"What precisely were you practicing? Putting, chips?"

"I hit my driver some. With the practice ball. Then I was using my nine iron."

"And when do you think the girls came by? What time?"

"It was dark. I heard Angela singing. Have you heard her sing?"

I nodded.

"She can sing anything. She can even sound like Prince. That was around eight-thirty, I think. But they didn't stay long. Angela wanted to be home by nine to see some dumb show. So she left."

"What were you talking about—with the two of them?"

"The usual stuff. School. Our crappy science teacher. What a shit that guy is. Lindsay wanted to try my clubs."

"And did you let her?"

"I let her play with the putter. I didn't want her using the driver. It was too long for her anyway."

"And then?"

"Angela went home like I told you."

"And Lindsay stayed."

"Yeah. She started fooling around with the driver. Swinging it around. I told her to cut it out."

"And did she?"

"She chucked it to one side." He looked surprised. "Maybe I didn't bring it in. I thought I did. I told the police I did," he said with a worried look at his grandfather.

"That's all right," Alex said.

"So she put the club down and then?"

"She started asking me if I liked these dumb groups. I said I had to go in."

"You went inside before she left?"

"Yeah. Lindsay was always bugging me. She never knew when you're bored. Know what I mean? It was too dark anyway for golf, and the *Batman* movie was going to be on."

"Did you see her leave?"

"She was walking across the lawn. Then I went in. I didn't think it was, like, important."

"Understandably," I said. "Now can you tell me anything else about Lindsay? You said she was bugging you. What does that mean?"

"You know. Girlfriend stuff. She wanted to go out to the movies and hang around the park."

"I see. She liked you."

"I dunno," he said, making me think he had some of his grandfather's caution. "She wanted a boyfriend. No way!"

"Why not?"

"Girls are boring. Most of them anyway," he added, as if he were a fundamentally truthful child. "I got sick of listening to Lindsay. Blah, blah, blah."

"You knew her fairly well? You'd been her neighbor for several years?"

"Yeah. But I never played with her. She ran around with the girls when we were little."

"Do you know what she was interested in—besides gymnastics?"

"She wasn't interested in anything besides gymnastics. And dumb groups."

"Who were were her friends?"

He shrugged. "Patsy. Patsy Culver is in the gymnastics club. There's a couple others that go to gymnastics, but I don't really know them. She hung around with Angela in the neighborhood."

"She liked Angela?"

"Yeah."

"And did Angela like her?"

Scott appeared to be giving this some thought. "She wanted to be like Angela," he said. "She was always running after her. Dressed like her, talked like her. She wanted a boyfriend like Angela. She was kinda dopey, Lindsay. A jock, you know."

"So Angela has a boyfriend?"

Scott gave a sly smirk. "You betcha."

"Anyone you know?"

"Everybody wants to know about Angela," Scott said with satisfaction. "Angela is something else."

"In what way?"

Scott shrugged, His blocky features puzzled. "Angela is, like, older," he said at last. "Angela isn't like anyone else at all."

SEVEN

THE VALONS' HOUSE wasn't more than two hundred yards from the Ursons', so I decided to stop by. I doubted I'd have another chance to visit Bradley and Sidonie. Our train left quite early in the morning, and I planned to go back with Harry and return to work. I'd told Alex Valon that there was nothing much to be done until the police got the report on the club. With luck, there'd be fingerprints other than Scott's. Unless his, and possibly Lindsay's, were the only prints, all that was against the boy was a reputation for breaking glass and the misfortune of being the last person known to have seen the deceased. "Worrisome," I'd told Alex, "but not fatal."

"That's what Tosh said. Tosh Stoughton, the local police chief."

"It's all right to overreact when it's your grandchild." I'd patted his arm and told him to keep me informed. Across the lawn, a few trees in the little grove were coming into flower. I'd go home and take up fraud, finagling, and bodyguard assignments and set aside questions of motive and opportunity. Still, it would be interesting to know who could have seen Lindsay walking home, and from which, if any, of these wide-spaced houses one could watch the Valons' front yard. It would be interesting, too, to know the Sunday night whereabouts of each of the Estates' residents. But the police would already be onto that, sifting through the transcripts of tedious house-to-house interviews. I wondered if Ken had ever corrected his statement, why he'd told me the story in the first place, and whether it was true that he'd left the compound.

I stopped beside the grove and looked back. The upper story of the Valons' house was visible. But someone watching from there would scarcely have had time to go downstairs and across the yards in time to kill Lindsay. Perhaps someone else had passed by earlier and seen the girls and Scott or appeared immediately after the boy went in. As I passed several deep beds of rhododendrons, azaleas, and hollies, I could understand why the police would focus on Scott despite his age—or William, if he had been out walking that night. The Estates' buildings were too far apart; there was too much cover and, consequently, too little chance of a witness. This was going to be a tough case.

The Ursons' house was an oversized brick Colonial with a fine-slate roof, a copper-topped porch and a brilliant red door that was opened by Caroline Urson. She was tall and fair like her father, but with her mother's good features and a lot of well-groomed blond hair. I apologized for coming so soon after the funeral and explained that her mother had asked me to stop by. "We're leaving first thing tomorrow."

Caroline Urson took all this in without comment, then said, "Mom's gone up to her room."

"Perhaps you could just tell her I stopped in—and explain about the train times?"

She nodded and started to close the door, when Sidonie called from upstairs, "Who is it, Caroline?"

"Some friend of the Brownings'."

"Anna Peters," I called. "I won't bother you now."

"Come in," she said. I could see a shadow move at the top of the stairs. "I told you about Anna, Caroline." She came downstairs, still in her black dress and heels, and her daughter stepped aside to let me in.

"Mom needs to rest," Caroline said.

"I'll only be a minute. It's just that we're leaving early tomorrow."

"So your husband told me," Sidonie said. "He brought the book over. The opening was very well attended."

"The opening was terrific, and you had everything planned perfectly. I know Harry enjoyed it. It turned out to be awfully good for him."

"Yes, I thought so. Of course, we didn't realize how ill he'd been when we decided on the artist."

"Well, we really appreciated it." I smiled awkwardly and put my hand on the door, thinking to leave.

"Don't go just yet," Sidonie said. "Come in for a moment. I want to talk to you."

"Mom," said Caroline.

Sidonie gave her a look and she shrugged angrily.

"In here," Sidonie said, opening the door to a small, beautifully paneled library with floor-to-ceiling bookcases and a great many leather-bound books.

"This is nice," I said.

"Thank you. I designed this. I did the whole house, in fact. I wanted to be a decorator."

"I'd say you were very good."

She gave a small, bitter smile. "I decided I wanted to be home with the children, but really I lacked confidence. And Bradley liked me home. We have to entertain a lot."

"I'm sure you do that well, too, if the gallery is any indication." I was uncomfortably aware that I didn't know what to say.

"The gallery has been wonderful. Meeting fascinating people. Being responsible for the shows. I probably spent too much time there."

"You weren't at the gallery when it happened. You mustn't blame yourself for that."

"You know, Bradley has always been obsessed with safety," she said. "We have all the latest security devices, electronic windows—I was always setting them off. It's funny, we have everything to keep us safe but him. I'm home and he's—" She covered her mouth as if to keep back the words. "I'm sorry," she said after a minute. "I don't know why I'm going on."

"It's all right. I'd guess it's because I'm a stranger, and I'm leaving tomorrow."

"Everybody wants me to talk about it. I'm not sure I want to. Everyone says it would be good for me."

"Maybe not," I said. "People are different."

"That's what I try to tell Isabel. She's been very kind, but—"

"Isabel might well spend some more time with Angela," I said more tartly than I'd meant. Maybe the distinctive Branch Hill atmosphere was getting me down.

"We never spend enough time with our children. I realize that now. All the cliches of 'they're only young such a short time'—they're true. But you never think you won't have time."

"No."

"Lindsay needed more time," she said. "She didn't know what she wanted yet. Or who she wanted to be or what she wanted to do. She was still too impressionable."

I wanted to ask who she'd been impressed with, but my better nature made me say, "I should tell you one thing."

She looked up.

"Alex Valon has asked me to investigate what happened. Because of Scott. He's worried about the police questioning the boy."

"I see."

"Alex is an old friend. I used to do work for his insurance company and we've always gotten along well. He's naturally upset."

"I always thought detectives snooped around without warning. I thought that was the point."

"Sometimes it is. But in this case, I've been staying with friends of yours; you and Harry worked on the show; most important, Lindsay was your child. I want everything to be up front."

"It doesn't matter to me," she said, distressed. "I don't know why you thought it would matter to me."

"It was just a courtesy. No implications. No warnings."

She jumped up. After a minute she said, "I know that. I don't know why I'm being nasty."

"It's not the time to talk about anything."

"Except this," she said. "I want Lindsay's murderer caught, and I don't care who catches him. And I don't care who it is or who gets hurt. Don't expect me to protect anyone. You can tell Alex and Dottie that."

"They're not asking for anything," I said. "Alex is completely convinced his grandson is innocent. And I'm convinced there's not much evidence against the boy. I really don't think I'm going to be involved. Of course, if there's any proof one way or the other, it has to be made public. Alex understands that."

Sidonie had walked over to the window and begun fiddling with the cord on one of the blinds. "I don't think I can stay here now," she said. "I don't think I can."

I could understand that.

"I don't think I can live the way I used to live. You know I did a lot for the children's sake. I won't be able to do that now."

"And your husband?" I asked. I wondered if he, too, was disillusioned with Branch Hill, with exclusive communities, with protection and control.

"I'm going to leave Bradley. They'll all be shocked," she said calmly. "I've hinted to Isabel, but she only hears what she wants to hear. I simply have to get out. Someone around here killed my daughter. One of these people Bradley's so impressed with killed my child."

Her fingers trembled on the cord, and I could see the tears on her face.

"Can I get you something?" I asked. "Shall I have Caroline come in?"

"No," she said. "I'd rather be alone. I've hardly been able to breathe between her and Isabel. I'd appreciate it if you'd go out by the back door, so she won't know you're gone."

"All right, if you're sure," I said, getting up to leave.

"Oh, I'm sure." She spoke with poisonous serenity. I was at the door before she said, "You'll tell me, too, won't you? If you find out anything."

Strictly speaking I couldn't agree to any such thing, but I found myself nodding. "If I find who killed her, yes. But nothing else."

"There's nothing else in this world I want to know," she said.

THERE WAS AN herb garden behind the Ursons' house, all laid out with brick paths. A few of the plants were still in flower, and late bees were flying around the beds with manic intensity. There was an ornamental fence all around the garden proper and around a small patch of the enormous lawn beyond, as though either Sidonie or Bradley had found the lack of boundaries disconcerting. To get out, I had to use a small gate partway down the garden, and I had just closed it and started around the side of the house when I heard voices from the garage.

". . . I'm disappointed. Goddamn disappointed in you."

"I'm trying to tell you. There was no way. The cops have been after me morning and night."

"The police managed to get to the funeral. Wilson and Canelli and the other detective. They were there. Where the hell were you? Or was that too much to ask?"

"Jesus! Everyone's on my ass! I'm fucking sick of it, man. I can't go anywhere without taking crap. The cops've been over a dozen times. I come home, there they are. The Gores are going to throw me out, I know they are. I don't know what I'm going to do. Shit, I'm sorry, but I don't know what I'm going to do."

Bradley's voice—I recognized it now—turned concerned, avuncular. "We can work something out about that. What have I told you? You've got people on your side. Right? Listen, if I had the slightest doubt, would I be talking to you? Would I? Does that make sense?"

I heard a sulky mumble.

"The only thing is the car. I must remind you of that."

"There wasn't anything with the car. I told you. It was in the garage by ten. Damn Davis has the plate number, everything."

"If you'd gone to the concert as you'd said—"

"I just changed my mind, that's all. I got halfway to New Haven and said the hell with it. I hate to go alone and the band sucks anyway."

Bradley Urson's voice had a wide range of expression. Next up was arctic blast. "You never intended to go to the concert."

"That's a lot of shit."

"I drew the line at drugs. You know that."

"I'm clean. I swear! That was the agreement, wasn't it? If I went to the Gores and everything?" He sounded nervous, a step from desperation.

"If you'd gone to the concert," Bradley said relentlessly, "you wouldn't have been home until the early hours."

"Don't I fucking know it! But listen—listen, for once I'm clean. And what happens? The cops think—"

"Everyone's uptight," Bradley said. "Everyone feels it. I just wanted to know. And I wanted you at the service. How's that going to look, for God's sake?"

"Look? I could be charged with murder. Who the hell cares about looks?"

"You'd better," Bradley said. "The position you're in now, you'd better. I'm thinking of you. I thought I could rely on you. That's important, you know." There was a note of appeal in his voice.

I stepped onto the drive and saw them. Bradley was standing with one hand on William's shoulder. "I'll go to bat for you," Bradley was saying, "but I've got to feel I can rely on you."

"Yeah, oh, yeah," the boy said. "You can. Really, you can."

"Hello, Bradley. William," I said. The two men looked at me blankly. "Anna Peters. Sidonie asked me to stop and say good-bye. We have to leave early tomorrow."

"Oh, yes," Bradley said, shifting into the correct gear. "We really appreciated your staying for the service. People have been so kind. The Madrigal Society—"

"Beautiful music," I said.

"Yes. You're leaving tomorrow, you said?"

"Yes." I put out my hand. "Harry and I are terribly sorry. I wish there was something we could do."

"Thank you. But we have to pick up the pieces," he said. "I've been trying to tell Sidonie and William here. You have to pick up the pieces and go on. We've too much invested to give up. That's what I tell them."

I shook his hand and nodded to William, who still seemed uncertain who I was. As I walked down the drive, I heard Bradley say, "We need to talk. You understand that? We need to talk seriously. Maybe go get a burger. How's that?"

I could not hear William's reply, but as I was going into the Brownings' I saw Bradley and William leave in the car. Bradley was betting on William's innocence. Betting very heavily by the look of it, and I wondered if he had any reasons for his confidence.

I FOUND HARRY ASLEEP upstairs, his sketchbook open beside him on the bed. I pulled the quilt over him and went downstairs to make a cup of coffee. I was just pouring the water when Isabel came in. "How was Sidonie?" she asked without preliminary. "Harry'd said you were going to stop by."

I shrugged. "Okay, I guess. Pretty good all being considered."

"I'm just on my way there now. I don't think she should be alone."

"Sidonie said she was going to rest. She was just going up when I left."

"Oh," Isabel said and frowned slightly.

"Caroline's there anyway," I said. "And Bradley should be back pretty soon."

"Bradley? Wasn't he home?"

"He was going out for a burger with William."

"William wasn't at the service," Isabel said. "I'm not sure he should have been under the circumstances, but still—Bradley's spent a lot of time with him."

"What's wrong with William?"

"I'm not too sure. Drugs, I suppose, or alcohol. He seems disconnected somehow. He dropped out of the Rhode Island School of Design, got thrown out at home, bummed around. I'm not fond of Bradley, but he stepped into a difficult situation. The boy was actually living from hand to mouth. He got into some sort of fight, a street fight, and Bradley stepped in. Not everyone would have done that—I've got to give Bradley credit for that. Anyway, after that William stayed with them a few weeks and then got the job driving for the Gores."

"Nice of them, too."

"I don't know about that—they pay him next to nothing. He does the yard and so on. Apparently he's seemed okay, just a bit muddled sometimes."

"Still a tendency to get into fights?"

"I think he's been hassled even here. There's something odd about William that doesn't bring out the best. I find myself thinking I'm glad Angela hardly knows him."

"Lindsay must have known him," I said. "If he stayed in their house."

"Lindsay never took much interest in her dad's projects."

"No?"

"He devotes his life to the walking wounded. It seems kind of crazy to me. I mean, good works are wonderful and socially useful but it's not much of a life, is it? And with two daughters—"

"Yet Bradley is very security conscious. Almost unreasonably so."

"Oh yes. They have all the latest. I remember Sidonie telling me. She thought it was a bit funny," Isabel said. "She said it was like living in Fort Knox."

"She seems a nice person."

"She's a marvelous person. All the charm in the world."

"And who did Lindsay take after?"

Isabel frowned at this. "It's hard to say. It sounds terrible, but Lindsay didn't have much personality. She never had anything to say. She just wasn't a kid who was socially adept. You probably noticed how she tagged along after Angela. Angela used to get a bit annoyed. She used to complain that Lindsay was sort of babyish. Well, you know how kids are."

"In fact, Lindsay was what, a half year older?"

"You'd never have known. I guess she was unsure of herself, except in gymnastics, where she was quite talented. I went to a couple of meets with Sidonie. She always went to see Lindsay perform."

"And Bradley?" I asked.

"Bradley's a very busy man," Isabel said.

"I'M PUZZLED," I said to Harry later. "Nobody seems to have known the kid. Even her mother goes on about how Lindsay hadn't known what she wanted or what sort of person she wanted to be. Isabel thinks she lacked personality. Angela thought she was babyish and denies they were special friends. Scott couldn't tell me much more than that she wanted to be like Angela."

"She sounds a bit dull," Harry agreed. "Poor kid. This place demands a certain luster, doesn't it? All these top-drawer communities and quality schools have expectations."

"Sure. But someone felt strongly enough about Lindsay to strike her three or four times, then stab her with the broken end of the golf club. That suggests other things."

"Like the neighborhood psycho."

"But she hadn't been sexually molested. That doesn't fit the usual pattern. No, something's missing here."

"You could stay and find out what."

"And you'd go back to cheeseburgers, french fries, and pie with ice cream. No. I told Alex: only if it was absolutely essential. And I'm sure it won't be. I'm sure they'll find prints or something and you'll be kept on your diet."

While Harry expressed himself on this point, I got dressed for dinner, and we were ready to go downstairs when the phone rang. A minute later, Isabel came up to say that Alex was on the phone. "Any news?" I asked him.

"Yes. Tosh just called me. The fingerprint experts are finished."

"And?"

"Nothing. Wiped clean, they think. Not a single usable print."

"I see. Well, we'd hoped for better, but it's certainly not the worst outcome."

"Not at all. You don't imagine a fourteen-year-old coolly cleaning up—you just don't."

"No," I said, although to my mind if you can think of murder, you can think of just about anything.

"I imagine they'll pull in the Brighton kid for questioning. He's an odd bird, one of those fellows who seem to attract trouble. Bradley Urson should have his head examined with some of the kids he's picked up. The thing is, it seems Brighton was in the Estates that night. Apparently he borrowed the Ursons' car. That's what I've heard."

"You heard correctly. He'd told Bradley he wanted to go to a concert in New Haven, but apparently he came back early—by ten."

"The times are right, then. You know, Anna, I feel so much better already. It was silly to worry. I just hope Scott doesn't feel I distrusted him."

"I'm sure he was glad you were on his side when the police came around."

"Yes, I think so. And you, too. I appreciate your advice. I spent my working life telling people to slow down and work things out logically, but when it's your own—"

"Alex, I've just gone through that myself. Minor problems happen to other people."

He laughed for the first time since Lindsay's body had been discovered. "You're so right," he said. "Thanks again, Anna. Now go home and take care of that talented husband of yours."

EIGHT

THE HURRICANE SEASON arrived in D.C. with gray, impenetrable sheets of rain that slid monotonously down my office windows. Inside, air-conditioning chilled the spongy tropical air, as I arranged protection for well-heeled paranoids and for V.I.P.s anxious to fend off grievances, justifiable or not. Yesterday, it had been a minor sheik and a rising congressman; today, a developer just this side of legality and a nervous gent of mysterious income. "I feel as if I am gradually sliding onto the wrong side of the law," I said to Harry when I got home. "Some of those birds damn well ought to be nervous."

"You're just bored," my husband said, pedaling virtuously on his exercise bicycle.

"I suppose. And I shouldn't be. We have a lot to be thankful for."

"Count your blessings, as my mother used to say."

Harry's mom had shifted her base of operations to a retirement community near St. Pete. At the price of a week's visitation, I had gained fifty-one weeks of freedom, and I wasn't complaining. "I never fully appreciated your mother's wisdom," I said. "If I remember right she is also fond of 'Into each life a little rain must fall.'"

Harry laughed easily. "Do you know I'm up to five miles a day? I'll be ready for the streets by spring."

"You've done very well. You look better than you did before you took sick—no kidding."

"I'm starting to get ideas for paintings again. Something small this time. I think the gallery is right—large is nice, but small sells."

He seemed so pleased that I said, "How lucky you are never to be bored by your work."

"There are days," he said, looking at me shrewdly. "You just hate routine. It's surprising you're any good at business."

"Baby is a demon for details. And so's Maxie. If anything, things run too smoothly."

"Did you see your mail? I brought in everything. It's over on the table."

"Most likely bills," I said, flipping through the pile. "We could save the rain forest by banning this junk."

"No offers you can't refuse?"

"No, but here's a letter from Alex Valon. There must have been some break in the Urson case." I opened the envelope and read the letter quickly. Behind me, Harry's cycle maintained a steady purr.

"How are they doing? Was it the nice musician with the pretty garden?"

"They don't know," I said, sitting down on the couch. "Or, rather, it sounds as if they can't decide."

"It's been months."

"Yes—and a limited group of suspects, excellent police work, the whole thing. But from what Alex says, no breaks at all. And everybody in the Estates has either been cleared or has an alibi or has been otherwise ruled out—except William, Bradley's protege, and Scott."

"Tough on old Valon."

"He's upset. He says he'd wanted to send Scott to a new school, but no go. The boy was rejected as soon as the principal made the connection. 'Temperature around town just over zero, Cynthia no help and Dottie worried.' He wants me to come 'have a look around,' as he puts it, and says he trusts my 'inimitable ability to stir up trouble.' I'm not sure that's a compliment."

"You ought to go. It'll be as good as a vacation for you. It'll *be* a vacation for you."

"I don't know."

Harry got off his bike, wiped his face with a towel, and sat down beside me. "You can't worry about me forever," he said. "I'm as fine as I'm ever going to be. That's pretty good, and even if it wasn't, we can't live as if I might keel over at any moment. For one thing, it gets on my nerves."

"It's not that," I said, although of course it was. "You seem fine to me."

"I *am* fine and you should start treating me as fine. You're too damn nervous about me."

"I guess. It's habit, you know. You get in the habit of worrying, of being alert, of—I suppose, of preparing for the worst."

"It was a rough six months," he said, stroking my head affectionately. "You took good care of me. But now you've got to realize I'm well."

"And give you a little more room?"

"Just a little."

"Enough to go to Branch Hill and see if I can help Alex out?"

"I think that would be just enough—provided you're not away too long. I don't want you away too long." He stood up and slung his towel around his neck. "I'm going to get a shower," he said.

"I'll start dinner."

"Don't start anything yet. I'm fine in *every* way. And then we'll go out to dinner."

"That's two good ideas," I said.

"Here's another one: call Alex and tell him you're coming up to make some trouble."

CONNECTICUT WAS bright and clear, and Branch Hill seemed very small and tidy after the contrasting opulence and squalor of the capital. "This place always looks as if the cleaning squad has just gone through," I said to Alex.

"Yes, it's well maintained." He turned his silver Mercedes onto the main street. "But how long that will last, I don't know. The budget will pinch even here."

"Hard to believe it from the look of the place."

"Appearances are deceiving," he said bitterly. "I don't feel the same about Branch Hill anymore. It has the defects of its qualities."

"Which are?"

"Malice with taste, cruelty with restraint, and deceit with a smile."

"Sounds almost Shakespearean."

"You know, Anna, I worked more than thirty years in the insurance business, a business where appearances matter a good deal. I think you'd agree?"

"Sure thing."

"But a good company, or a good person, has substance underneath. Your reputation used to be important, because it was the ultimate guarantee of your company. Not the other way around."

"And Branch Hill?"

"Branch Hill is capable of deceit. Someone knows, Anna. I'm beginning to think that more than one person knows. Don't tell me—paranoia is to be avoided."

"No, I suspect you're right. Or to be kinder, one person knows and others suspect but aren't sure or have no proof."

"Or can't face the unpleasantness of accusing a friend or neighbor or one of the pillars of the community?"

"That's not just Branch Hill. Ask any cop."

"I can hardly speak to police now. They seem content to leave Scott in limbo, under the worst of suspicion. I think they phoned the school."

"The boarding school you were looking at?"

"Yes. Though Tosh denied it, he looked uncomfortable. I think one of the detectives phoned. They want him here, where they can keep an eye on him. It's damnable! He's only fourteen years old!"

"And William—Brighton, was that his name?"

"Brighton. They'd do better to keep an eye on him," Alex said in agitation. "I understand he's gotten a little job at the photo store."

"He's still living in town, then?"

"Yes and no. I've heard he's been house-sitting. Here and around. I imagine that's the only sort of work he can get."

"I imagine."

Alex pulled up in front of a handsome old house with bow windows and a multitude of dormers. "I thought you'd like this better than one of the motels," he said. "The Seafarer's Inn, Bed and Breakfast."

"Very nice."

"We'll get you set here and then a car."

"I can manage that, Alex, if you're busy."

"I'm retired now. And, as you might guess, I'm not quite so busy with the community anymore."

I could have bitten my tongue. "I'm sorry."

"It's just the way people are. So. I'm at your service."

"Well, I'll need to pay a courtesy call on the police. Perhaps see your friend Tosh?"

"Tosh Stoughton. I'll call him."

"All right. But be prepared for him to be awkward. They don't always like private investigators."

"He'll have to put up with it," Alex said.

"And something else you could do—get me a good town map and something that shows the Estates. I mean every house in the Estates."

"I can get photocopies from Town Hall."

"Good. I'll want you to go over them with me and label all the Estate houses."

"Is there anything else you'll need?"

"Just addresses. I think maybe Sidonie Urson has moved."

"That's right! The scandal of the last six weeks. Dottie'll know where she's gone." He gave me a sharp look. "How'd you know about that?"

"She told me she was going to leave the Estates. I gathered it was to be without Bradley."

"Yes, although they're both gone. He's put the house on the market. It'll take a while to sell, the way property is moving at the moment."

"Why don't you call Tosh from here and drop me off in town if he can see me? Then if you could pick up those maps and call about a car, I'll be set as soon as I'm finished with the police."

"Fine," said Alex, lifting my case out of the trunk. "I'll just introduce you to Mrs. Weaver first. Admire the stenciling, which is her pride and joy, and you'll get on fine with her."

The Seafarer's Inn was the last word in comfort and elegance, Branch Hill's riposte to generations of modest British rooms with shared baths. I had an immense room on the second floor, replete with antique furniture, good prints, and a view of the marina and the river. Harry would have loved it, and I regretted that I hadn't persuaded him to come along as a little vacation. Perhaps I ought to call him, I thought, then caught myself: Harry needed to be on his own and maybe I did, too. I went downstairs, told Alex the place was perfect, and suggested that we get started.

THE POLICE DEPARTMENT occupied the ground floor of the Town Hall, and while Alex went upstairs to look out the maps, I presented myself to Branch Hill's finest, complete with license and identification.

"That's all right," said the chief. He had white hair, a blunt, red, Irish face, and the remains of a genial disposition. "To tell you the truth, I'm glad to see you. Alex has been driving us crazy. If you can clear the kid, more power to you. We've devoted literally tens of thousands of man hours to this case, and whatever we may think privately, we haven't enough to make an arrest."

"But enough to keep the case open."

"Murder cases are always open. This is the first murder in town since the eighteenth century. Since before Branch Hill was incorporated, as the mayor likes to remind me. The perpetrator was either very clever or very lucky. Or both."

"Have you been worried that there might be other killings? Has that been one of the concerns?"

"To hear my fellow citizens discuss it, you'd think that was the only concern. But no. It's been too long and the case doesn't fit the profile of a serial killer."

"That had been my impression. But if she was chosen deliberately—"

"Where's the motive?"

"Yes, granted I was only here a short while, but I never got any clear sense of Lindsay Urson's personality."

"You've put your finger on it. She was a good kid—no drink, no drugs, no boyfriends. Hell, she spent too much time in the gym to get into trouble, and that's a fact. Her name was up on all the practice schedules and the gymnastics instructors say she never missed. She was at the center every day right after school until five o'clock and all day Saturday. Sunday was her family's day to visit the grandparents, go out for a big brunch, that sort of thing. Summers, she went to gymnastics in the morning and to the pool in the afternoon, then to summer camp—gymnastics camp."

"Anything there?" I asked. "What about steroids, growth retardants? Top gymnasts all look so tiny and immature you have to wonder—"

"We checked that angle: nothing. And all the gymnastics school personnel, too. Every one of them is straight, upright, clean as a whistle."

"It certainly sounds as if something is missing," I said.

"That's my feeling. But what? We've checked out all past and present residents of the Estates. We've checked out every one of Bradley Urson's social projects: The Brighton kid was the only one in the area. He hasn't got an alibi, but there's no evidence against him except his troubled background."

"Like Scott Cushing," I said.

"Oh, there's a little more against Scott," he said. "The club, for one thing. Proximity, for another."

"But no prints," I said.

"No nothing," said the chief, standing up to signal that our conversation was over. "But I'm patient. Sooner or later the killer will make a mistake or someone will tell us what we need to know. A town like this, someone always knows." He gave a tight, rather disagreeable smile and held the door open for me.

In the outer office, Chief Stoughton introduced me to the two detectives in charge of the case, Burt Wilson, big and clever-looking with fashionable hair, and Mike Canelli, small and neat with large, mild eyes and a bored expression. After shaking their hands and promising my cooperation, I went outside to the parking lot. Alex was in the car reading the evening paper, several photocopied maps beside him on the seat. "I thought we'd drive home first," he said. "Dottie will be able to tell you Sidonie's address and then I'll take you round to pick up the car."

Though I'd have preferred my own transport, I said that was fine. At the Valons' house, only Dottie was home, and after I'd added Sidonie's—and Bradley's—new addresses to my notebook, I unfolded the map of the Estates on the coffee table. I traced the main drive and found the curve before the Brownings' house. "This is the Brownings'?"

Alex squinted nearsightedly, but Dottie said, "That's right. And here's ours, number seven."

I labeled the houses.

"The Ursons are next," she said. "It's such a shame about them. And they won't get what they paid for the house. Not with the market as it is."

"And whose is this?" I pointed to a house set diagonally to the other two—the only one that overlooked the Valons' side yard.

"Can you see that, Dottie? It's these new glasses," Alex complained. "Something like this is just the wrong distance away."

"Alex has done nothing but complain since he had to get bifocals," Dottie said. "That's the Ems—number eleven. I think you met them at the service. And behind them, the Gores—where that crazy boy was staying. Unbelievable! Fortunately, Nancy Gore put her foot down on that."

Maybe not soon enough, I thought. If William had been walking from the Ursons' garage back to the Gores, he surely would have seen Lindsay. Had he gone directly back, and if he hadn't, where had he been? I wondered if the police had cleared that up.

"Then you have the Montanis. Isn't it the Montanis, Alex?"

"No, they're at number eighteen. I'd better check," Alex said and went off for the phone book. Dottie and I had most of the rest by the time he came back with the information.

"Thanks," I said, when the last names were penciled in. "If Alex can drop me down at the car rental—"

"You'll be back for dinner," Dottie said.

"No, I think I'll pick up something quick in town and get started. I want to talk to as many people as I can, as soon as I can."

"Anna is always very conscientious about not running up a bill," Alex said dryly. We'd negotiated on a couple of those for Independence Mutual.

"In compensation for the extraordinary expenses," I teased, "but really, I want to get busy before word gets around."

"Oh, yes," said Dottie, the picture of innocence. "It's surprising how news gets passed around even in a place the size of Branch Hill."

NINE

I MISSED Bradley Urson. "Thursday's Mr. Urson's day for the Teen Center Board," his secretary told me, in a snippy, impatient tone that suggested I should have known better. Friday didn't look to be any better for his schedule, and everything was "very tight until the middle of next week." I decided to try him later at home. I had better luck with Sidonie. She was just leaving the gallery when I called, but agreed to see me around seven. I said I'd find the way, and after sampling what was promised as "the shoreline's best pizza," I reached her condo before the sun went down. It was in a big, sparsely tenanted new complex, a small city of shingled New England cottages stretched to three- and four-story height, all squashed together on a narrow lot across the street from a tidy new marina. I negotiated a maze of postmodern angles, Palladian windows, and miniscule decks and balconies to Sidonie's building and went up two flights permeated by the acrid smell of new synthetics. The place was spotless and felt empty, but when Sidonie Urson opened her door, I saw the advantages. Across the foyer and the living room, a line of big windows overlooked the river's mouth and the Sound. Nothing was visible but water and sky, as if one were standing on the very edge of the continent.

"This is spectacular," I said.

"That's everyone's reaction. Though not everyone likes the effect."

"I gather the units have been selling slowly."

"They overbuilt for the market. In fact, I picked this up at auction. But there'll be some more tenants soon. A number of us took advantage of the bargains."

"Will that be good? Or not so quiet?"

"Not so quiet. Come in and sit down. Don't mind the debris," she said, clearing away the cartons from a Chinese dinner. "I've decided I hate cooking."

"It's never been my favorite, either."

"I almost asked if you'd like to eat out somewhere, but then I wasn't sure how this interview might go."

"I understand. I'm sure the delays and uncertainty have been very hard."

"Oh, I'm quite certain about some things." She made a vague gesture that encompassed the apartment.

"You didn't seem surprised to hear I'd come back north."

"I expected that all along," she said.

"And you've decided to stay in Branch Hill?"

"The gallery's here."

"And friends."

"And whoever killed my daughter," she said with the first edge to her chilly serenity. "Don't forget that."

"The reason for my trip."

She shrugged. "The police seem very thorough. Tosh Stoughton tells me they just need a break. They need a break to be sure which one."

"I'll be honest with you: I think there's still something that hasn't been accounted for yet."

"Like what?"

"I don't know. I need to know more about Lindsay before I'll know that. I was hoping you could tell me some other things about her. About her friends, her interests, the people she was attracted to—that sort of thing."

"You know she was interested in gymnastics? Seriously interested?"

"Tosh Stoughton said she was at the gym all afternoon every afternoon and all day Saturdays."

"Yes. I used to worry. To tell you the truth, I thought it was too much for her. I don't mean physically; physically, she was super for athletics. Strong joints, good muscles, very few injuries. But I sometimes had the feeling that her whole life had narrowed down to the gym. All she did was practice and go to meets. She wasn't developing socially at all."

"I gather that's the fate of precocious athletes."

"Well, I had a talk with Sue Tansi—she runs the gymnastics program. You know, to see if Lindsay was Olympic material, to see if there was a real point to—well, giving up everything else."

"And?"

Sidonie winced slightly. "Sue was very candid. She said Lindsay could go to one of the best collegiate gymnastics programs in the country, that she'd possibly get scholarship offers. But as for international competition, no. She predicted, looking at Bradley and me, that Lindsay would get too big. She did have a tendency to put on weight, even training as hard as she did, and in any case, the very top level just wasn't in the cards for her."

"Did your daughter know that?"

"Sue said Lindsay was very realistic about her abilities." Sidonie gave a rueful smile. "She said the athletes are usually more realistic than their parents."

"I'm sure."

"I suppose it follows. But Sue was also concerned. I'll do her justice—Sue can be absolutely brutal about questions of talent, but she's very tactful in other areas—she said that she was worried. Like me, she felt Lindsay was using gymnastics as a way to avoid other things."

"Like what?"

"Growing up. School social life. More contact with her peers. It was an escape for her. Not just the sport itself, but the routines, the schedules, the whole little cultish world."

"She was shy?"

"Yes, and immature. I really think she was immature rather than limited. She did quite well in school—Bs mostly, but a few As, too, although, you know, she never seemed clever. She was never one of those kids who can make jokes or come up with smart answers. Caroline, now, is full of fun. A take-charge sort of kid. Lindsay always hung back. She lacked confidence."

Sidonie stopped for a moment and looked down at her hands. "Somehow, Bradley and I didn't give her the sense that she was important. I tried, but she was one of those girls who need their father's attention."

"Your husband works a lot with children," I said carefully.

"Other people's children. Other people's *sons*. Lindsay felt that, but she was so quiet, so focused on the gymnastics, I didn't see it. Or maybe I didn't want to see it. Maybe that was it. Maybe it suited me fine. I've been asking myself that."

There wasn't really anything I could say, and after a minute she resumed. "That's why I was glad when she took up with Angela."

"This was recently?"

"The last year or so. Lindsay idolized Angela; it was one of those adolescent crushes. Lindsay was just at the point of caring about clothes. She used to want clothes like Angela's—all those dark things with long skirts like a Martha Graham dancer's. I'll admit they looked all right on Angela but they didn't suit Lindsay at all. I used to try to explain to her about style, about finding the style that suits you best. It was no use. I was annoyed at the time. Now I see it was because Angela was always so poised, so precocious. Far too precocious."

"In what way?"

"This was last year—the girls were thirteen. I came into the living room when they were sitting talking, and I heard Angela discussing contraception—in the most graphic detail. I was really taken aback, because I'd been encouraging Lindsay to pal around with her."

"And you think Angela had practical experience or just theoretical knowledge?"

"It didn't matter to me which! I thought I had a good relationship with my daughter. I thought I knew what was troubling her. I certainly didn't want her getting information like that from a neighbor's kid."

"Yes," I said. "And Angela. Was she fond of Lindsay? Did she confide in her?"

"Angela was definitely the leader. I don't know what her feelings were beyond liking to be the leader, the star. Lindsay looked up to her, admired her. I think Angela was gratified." Sidonie's voice was cold.

"You don't care for the girl. Was this just since the contraception business or is there another reason?"

"I wouldn't say I disliked her. I just came to think she wasn't a good influence on Lindsay."

"Was there a boyfriend lurking in the background? Someone older, perhaps?"

"It's funny that you should ask that. I thought so, although that was based on nothing. Angela strikes me as a child avid for experience. And not a very happy child, either."

"No?"

"Well, Ken is quite notorious. Everyone knows he runs around; adultery is a hobby with him, and in a small place, people talk."

"Angela seems very attached to Martha."

"She's lucky to have Martha. Isabel can be super, but she's never been interested in Angela. Or only in passing. Isabel likes to be able to brag about Angela's singing. Angela's looks. But for all that, Isabel knows nothing about music, can't tell Monteverdi from Mantovani and hasn't bothered to learn. Angela's had a strictly laissez-faire child rearing, while I was—" She broke off the thought and twisted her hands together. "I can't help it," she said after a moment. "It's terrible, but I can't help thinking: It should have been Angela. It shouldn't have been Lindsay at all."

THE SKY HAD gone dark by the time I left Sidonie's, and it took me a while to find where Bradley was living. Branch Hill was small but sprawling, and its older developments had lots of circles and cul-de-sacs to confuse the visitor. Bradley had acquired a house in one of the least fashionable of these, a small ranch with a carport and a lot of overgrown arborvitae. I recognized his Saab parked in the driveway beside an old Chevy as big as a battle cruiser, and I went up and rang the bell.

There were footsteps in the back of the house before the door opened, releasing a powerful smell of fresh paint. The youth in the doorway was thin with sharp, well-shaped features, wavy black hair, and light, startling eyes. I registered that he was as handsome as William but probably more energetic, for there was paint in a half dozen shades on his T-shirt and jeans. He had a roller covered with green paint in one hand. With the other he held the door.

"Yeah?"

"I'm looking for Bradley Urson. Have I gotten the right address?"

Without answering, he yelled over his shoulder. "Bradley! Someone to see you." Then he stepped aside so I could go in. "Watch the wet paint," he warned.

"Who is it?" Bradley called.

"I dunno."

"Anna Peters," I called. "We met last spring."

Bradley was frowning when he emerged from the back, wiping his hands on a rag. "We're rather busy at the moment," he began, then stopped, recognizing me. "Anna! Sorry. With all that's been going on, I didn't make the connection. How are you?"

He removed some more paint, then shook my hand.

"I couldn't make an appointment with your office, so I thought I'd take a chance and stop by. I can see I didn't pick the best time."

"Renovations go on forever," he said. "This is Greg Beloi. Greg's helping me put the place in order. Really a clever workman. I'd be lost without him."

Greg looked bored. This one seemed less lost than William, less volatile than Scott: a tougher, more cynical type altogether. I wondered what his difficulty was, or if he'd simply spotted opportunity with Bradley.

"I need to talk to Anna for a few minutes. Why don't you finish that wall and clean up? That will do for tonight."

"Okay. But I need gas."

Bradley took out his wallet and gave Greg a twenty dollar bill, which he folded and slid into his tight and tattered jeans. Then he went off with his roller, and Bradley led me across the living room to a small, dark study equipped with bookshelves and a desk.

"We haven't started in here yet. The paint smell isn't as bad." He switched on the desk lamp and shut the door. After the elegance of the Ursons' former library, the cramped little office with the fake paneling and acoustic tile represented quite a comedown. Bradley dropped into one of the vinyl chairs and said, "It's a bit of a mess now, but I think it'll be an okay investment. In the long run."

"The market's certainly slow at the moment."

"The market's dead at the moment. We're offering the house in the Estates for thousands less than we paid for it. Not a nibble."

"Sooner or later," I said.

"Oh, yes. Branch Hill is sound. If they were to put in a state income tax, we'd lose some of the New York money, but quality property in a fine suburban location will always hold its value." Bradley sounded like a Chamber of Commerce speech, and he surprised me by shaking his head in irritation as if he recognized the artificiality. "Of course you didn't come up from Washington to discuss property values."

"No. Alex Valon wrote and asked me to come."

"He's worried about Scott."

"Yes. And I've worked for Alex before—for Alex's company, actually."

"I see." In the shaded light, Bradley's fine-boned face was puffy and off-color. There were pouches under his eyes and new lines in his cheeks. Despite his good works, Bradley had been suspect and unpopular in some way with the Estates crowd, and everyone had focused on Sidonie's grief. His feelings had rather been discounted, I remembered, but the physical evidence told me just how hard the summer had been.

"I've promised to help. If I can. That means trying to find out all I can about Lindsay, about the neighbors, about Scott and William Brighton and whoever else might be involved."

Bradley didn't say anything.

"I'm sorry to have to intrude, but at this point any little detail might turn out to be important."

Bradley made a sound between a laugh and a sigh. "The police have two suspects. They've told you that?"

"Yes."

"I think they're content with that."

"Surely not. They can't close a case with two suspects."

"You'd be surprised. The town is surprisingly content, too. I thought there'd be outrage, civic unrest. I didn't know how things worked."

"What do you mean?"

"This town doesn't want to be disturbed."

"I should think having not one but two murder suspects in residence would disturb any place."

"So you'd think. But this way they don't have to be sure. You see that? There's just enough uncertainty. They make pariahs of the two boys—and dismiss anyone who speaks up for them—and go on without changing anything. They didn't care about Lindsay. They don't care about Scott. They've never cared about William." Bradley gave a bitter laugh. "William's fooled them. He's stayed on. They thought he would run and that would decide the police, but William's too smart. In his own way, he's very smart and very tough."

"Alex said he's working in a photo shop."

"Yes. I'd just gotten him started there before—he was an art major, graphics and photography, you know. He's very gifted, very sensitive." Bradley's voice was a monotone, as though he'd rehearsed William's virtues once too often. "Also a little prick, unfortunately. He didn't go to the funeral. I've hardly seen him since. And I could have helped him," he said with sudden energy. "My support might have cleared him entirely, but he felt it was too awkward. He felt he'd rather live in a shack."

"I didn't think Branch Hill had shacks."

"I exaggerate. The old marina has a boathouse with a little caretaker's apartment attached. William acts as night security in exchange for the room. He has a small darkroom there and he takes pictures of boats for the owners. He takes remarkably beautiful photos."

"That sounds more enterprising than I'd have imagined."

"He's better." Bradley smiled sourly. "William always saw himself as persecuted, as the misunderstood artist, as the rebel without a cause. Hard to maintain when your father runs Minder Chemicals."

"I can imagine."

"Now he really is an outcast. Now there really is prejudice against him, and I'm afraid he's thriving on it. William's been like an actor, practicing for a role that's finally materialized." Bradley rubbed a hand over his face. "You understand, he doesn't see the long-term consequences. He doesn't see how things could have been better. These kids—Greg's another one—they don't have imagination. They don't see the possibilities."

"And you try to help them see what's possible?"

"Yes, it's vitally important. These young men are the future, after all."

I thought that a future presided over by William and Greg might be curious. "And Lindsay?" I asked. "She was maybe too young to have had an idea of her future."

"She should have grown up, gotten married, had a family. I'm not so good with girls." He looked down at his hands and shrugged. "But Sidonie was a good mother. We never had a moment's trouble with either of them. Lindsay was good from the moment she was born." His face twitched. "She was a very pretty baby," he said.

"Was it just chance, then?"

"I don't know."

"You haven't mentioned Scott. Alex said you knew him well. Took a real interest in the boy."

"He had no father. No proper father. I don't know. I can't believe either one of them killed Lindsay. Scott is childish, if anything. I know—he looks sixteen or seventeen, but he's still interested in sports and video games, not girls. I remember last fall his showing me some firecrackers he'd gotten. He wanted to put them in the neighbors' trash cans. I talked him out of that, and we found a vacant lot and set them off. That's the sort of thing he was interested in. He needed attention. Alex has been great with him, of course, but Alex is his grandfather. He needed someone younger who could do things with him."

"He sometimes got into trouble."

"Trouble—Branch Hill trouble. A few broken windows. He liked golf and baseball—high-breakage sports."

"Ken told me he broke out every window in their garage. I got the impression that was deliberate."

"Ken had a thing with Cynthia. Of course the boy didn't like it." Bradley gave another disagreeable smile. "Don't believe everything the Brownings tell you. Isabel thinks Sidonie walks on water, and Ken says whatever he thinks will make him sound good. Believe me, I know. I've found out who my friends are."

"Am I correct in thinking William borrowed a car from you that night?"

"Yes. He had no car. I think he's got a bike now. During the day, the Gores let him drive their station wagon for errands and so on, but not at night. He told me he wanted to hear a concert up in New Haven."

"But he didn't go?"

"He says the car was back by ten."

"You weren't home until—eleven-thirty? He could have told you later and been in the clear."

"Davis had the plate number. The car was in at 9:48."

"What did William do then?"

"He says he saw no one was home, so he closed the garage and walked back to the Gores. Actually, I think he sat and smoked in the car—the ashtray was half full and the garage smelled of cigarette smoke."

"Was he waiting for someone?"

"I don't think so. I think he just didn't have anywhere else to go."

"No one saw him?"

"No."

I remembered the map: He could have avoided the grove by cutting through the Ursons' side yard. "Did Lindsay like William? Would she have called to him or waved if she'd seen him?"

"Lindsay didn't like William at all. She wouldn't even speak to him. The other kids in the area—Angela, now, she was always pleasant."

"Yes," I said. But I was thinking how odd it was that every conversation seemed to come back to Angela. Poor Lindsay had been the little girl nobody knew; Angela had been the focus of attention. As I said good night to Bradley, I thought I'd better move her to the top of my interview list.

TEN

I TRIED the Brownings' number when I got back to my plush accommodation in the Seafarer's Inn, but Ken and Isabel were at a party, Angela was still at a Madrigal Society rehearsal, and Martha, so she informed me, was shortly on her way to bed. I abandoned detection for the night, talked to Harry, and was abed at a righteous hour.

When I called the Brownings the next morning, Martha announced that this was Isabel's day for the League. I left my name for the second time and dialed the gymnastics center. There a brisk woman assured me that Sue Tansi was always busy but that before eleven would be best, because they had only their toddler, preschool, and Moms' Rhythmic Gymnastics programs in the mornings.

There were more rhythmic moms and well-coordinated toddlers than I'd imagined, for the long, narrow parking lot beside the Academy Gymnastics Center was nearly full. Inside the small foyer, a glass-fronted shop sold a variety of leotards, slippers, and warmup gear; beyond it was a locker area, several offices, and a big well-lighted gymnasium full of bright mats and lethal-looking apparatus. I ran my hand along a four-inch-wide balance beam and thought that whatever else Lindsay Urson might or might not have had in the way of personality, physical courage must have been included. The beam looked deadly; the vaulting horse, treacherous; the bars, suicidal. I was relieved to see that the toddlers were confined to the mats where they were threatening their tender necks and spines with only flips and somersaults, to the encouragements of the teacher and their overambitious mamas. Meanwhile, a variety of expensively turned out women were swirling red and blue ribbons to Scott Joplin music. The Chinese do these drills with casts of thousands. Branch Hill's was the capitalist version: competitive clothes and rhythmic anarchy. Between the jumping and hopping and the swinging of ribbons, they were all working up a sweat except for the small blond instructor, who had the professional's advanced musculature and unnatural stamina.

"All right, ladies," she said after a minute. She clapped her hands and they stopped, their streamers settling after them in languid loops and curls. "Jeanise! Can you take this group?"

A thin woman in a high-cut leotard trotted over, conferred briefly, then introduced the next exercise. Her colleague pulled on a pale blue warmup jacket and came to talk to me.

"I'm Sue Tansi," she said. "We're pretty full this morning, but I can take a break now."

"This is all a bigger operation that I'd imagined."

"The only way to pay the mortgage is to keep the building full. We try to offer a program for each and every individual." She gave me an appraising look. "Our rhythmic gymnastics and aerobics programs provide appropriate exercise for the less athletic."

"I'm afraid my idea of appropriate exercise is a not-too-brisk walk."

"A lot of people need the motivation of a group," Ms. Tansi said tactfully. She had a square, capable face and was a good deal older than her tiny, muscular figure suggested.

"No lack of motivation there," I said, nodding toward a boy of four or five, who was doing back flips with the help of the instructor.

"Some of them are quite fearless at that age."

"Too fearless for me."

She gave a soft laugh and opened her office door. "Now," she said, "what can I do for you? I have," she glanced at her watch, "maybe ten minutes."

"I want to know about Lindsay Urson. What sort of person she was, what sort of friends she had, whether anyone hung around the center waiting to see her."

"Never to the last," Tansi said.

"She was an unusually pretty girl. I thought maybe—"

"She was a beauty, but we're all business here and the kids, girls or boys, either come to work and work seriously or they don't come at all. That's understood."

"All right. Friends, then?"

"Patsy Culver. I'd say Patsy was her best friend. They used to sit together on the bus, spot for each other on exercises."

"Is Patsy in daily?"

"The team practices at four. You could see her for a few minutes then."

"Anyone else?"

"Rina Lipinski, maybe. Trish Goldberg. They were all the same age and on the team. Though neither of them is as good as Lindsay was."

"Was she your best gymnast?"

"Certainly the best at the moment. She was very dedicated. And very talented. Her only problem was her genetic inheritance. She was already a bit big and still growing. Gymnastics is like dancing: Many are called but few are chosen."

"Her mother said that she'd been a little worried about Lindsay's absorption in the sport."

"Yes, we talked about that and about her attitude. Success in sports usually gives girls confidence all around. Lindsay was the exception. She was driven— she really had a passion to excel, and she was totally poised in competition, solid as a rock. But somehow it didn't carry over."

"Any idea why not?"

Ms. Tansi shrugged. "Sidonie was tough competition, you know. Very elegant, very pleasant, very pretty. I think that without realizing it, she was a lot to live up to. And the father didn't take an interest. I suspect he was the one Lindsay was trying to impress. It's hard to say."

"Any odd changes in behavior—anything like that?"

"No, really nothing. We work here. I just see the girls in training situations." But even as she said that, she gave me a puzzled look. I waited, and then Ms. Tansi said, "There was one thing. It's so trivial that I don't think I've mentioned it before."

"What's that?"

"Someone came looking for Lindsay a day or so before she died. I didn't think anything of it. I know all the parents, of course, but once in a while we get family friends or relatives coming to pick up the students. For the little ones, I insist on a call beforehand. We can't be too careful, because we've had some nasty custody cases in Branch Hill. Anyway, a woman showed up and asked if she could speak to Lindsay. I wouldn't have thought anything of it, if she hadn't been unusual looking—very tall, striking, all in black with sunglasses."

"Incognito Countess."

Sue Tansi laughed. "Exactly."

"And Lindsay knew her?"

"They talked for no more than a minute. Lindsay seemed—upset is too strong a word. Disturbed, maybe. I asked if everything was all right, but she just hopped on the beam and went back to work. That's it." She smiled apologetically. "Now I really must go. The Rhythmic Gymnasts need a lot of encouragement."

"Thank you for your time."

"It was such a terrible thing. I'm sorry I can't be more helpful."

"You never know what will be useful," I said, although nothing seemed very pertinent. The case looked even more difficult than it had the last time I was in Branch Hill, and when I reached the parking lot, I decided to see if some appropriate exercise would give me inspiration.

The Academy was not far from the town center, and I soon reached the heavily yuppified collection of boutiques with clever names and imaginative prices. I loitered at an antique shop offering old sporting prints and made a note to buy one for Harry before I went home. I was admiring some good-looking sweaters in another window, trying to decide if I would wear a particularly pretty blue one often enough to justify its cost, when the reflection of a slim, dark girl with a great deal of hair slid by in the glass. I turned around and said, "Hello, Angela. I'd been planning to call you."

She gave a little start and blushed. It was just lunchtime on a weekday and she was in the center of Branch Hill, three miles from school. "Oh, hello," she said. "Mom mentioned you were back. We got out early today," she said. "Preparations for Founder's Day."

"Which is?"

"Commemoration of Hutchinson Morrison, our venerable founder. Now dead, of course."

"Which excuses your absence."

"More or less," she said.

"I used to take off a day or two myself at your age."

"And you survived."

"I ended up married at sixteen. Try to avoid that."

She colored a little and said nothing.

"Have you had lunch?"

Angela shook her head. "I'm not very hungry."

She was thinner than ever and rather pale. "I thought that the singer had to feed the voice. I'll treat, if money's a problem."

"All right," she said, but she didn't look very happy. "Maybe some yogurt."

"I thought it was pasta for the voice."

"Then you want Luigi's." She pointed across the street to a tiny one-story restaurant with awnings and windowboxes filled with chrysanthemums. It turned out to be as pretty inside as out and twice as refined. "I don't suppose they have plain spaghetti and meatballs," I said.

"The pasta with seafood is very good."

"We'll have that, if you'd like."

"Yes, all right," she said. She moved her fingers nervously as if food were an occasion for upsets and tensions. "Do you know what Maria Callas said?" she asked after we had ordered.

I shook my head.

"She said 'I lost my fat, then I lost my voice, then I lost Onassis.'"

"A lesson for you. Eat up."

"I think I might lose my voice," she said.

"Why is that?"

She shrugged and began to fiddle with the silverware. I decided not to press her and admired the immense bouquets and wreaths of everlastings that decorated the place. When we finished our soup, I said, "Is the Madrigal Society singing soon? I'd like to hear you."

"Next Friday. We're singing at the Congregational Church."

"Good. I may still be here."

"Are you going to talk to everyone again?"

"It's the only thing I can do. Sometimes people remember things. And sometimes they decide to tell things they haven't told before."

"Like what?"

"What they've seen. What they know. Sometimes why they feel bad." I looked at her and her large, intelligent dark eyes slid away like shy brown fish.

"Lindsay's not why I feel bad," Angela said. "It has nothing to do with Lindsay."

"Perhaps it has something to do with cutting school?"

"I find school very boring," she said in a supercilious tone that made me think she must be an uncomfortable pupil.

"Perhaps you feel too grown up for school."

"You think that's silly," she said.

"It's very likely not silly, though it may be shortsighted."

"Shortsighted?"

"You're clearly very talented. You could have a career in music if you keep at it. If you're willing to accept that discipline."

"If I'm willing to be a good girl and stay in school."

"Something like that. You need to stay in school anyway. You're not sixteen yet."

"Sometimes I feel a lot older," Angela said. She had made her way rapidly through most of a big plate of pasta. Now she began to play with her food, twirling the fettucini around and around with her fork.

"You'll feel older yet if you don't take care of yourself."

"What do you mean?"

"You're skin and bones. You started lunch as if you hadn't seen food in a week, but now you're reverting to a finicky eater. I'll bet you're driving your mom up the wall."

"She doesn't care," Angela said bitterly. "She's never around."

"Martha, then. You'll be worrying Martha."

"I get nervous," Angela said. "It's not deliberate or anything. I get nervous and then I can't eat. I'm not hungry."

"What are you afraid of?"

"Afraid?"

"You just said you get nervous. Of course, you live right next to Scott—"

"I'm not afraid of Scott," she said scornfully.

"Well, what about William Brighton, suspect number two? He's still around."

"You're like all the others. You're all wrong about William."

"Do you ever see him?"

"Oh, sure. He's around. It's not as if he has AIDS or something. Some of the kids—you know—they're not going to hang out with him. But I try to be nice to him. I always talk to him when I see him around."

"So it's not William. But still you've been afraid since Lindsay was killed. Isn't that right?"

"It was terrible. She was my friend, our neighbor."

I studied her without saying anything. Angela had one of those faces that never seems the same twice, an actress's face, stripped today and ready to assume a role. Her high, wide forehead suggested serenity and intelligence, an intellectual role; the severely pulled back hair, discipline and innocence; the eyes—the eyes, I thought, gave her away. She had a fanatic's eyes, alternately empty and burning: not at all what Branch Hill expected.

"You don't believe me," she said.

"No," I said, "not entirely. If I had to guess, I'd say you were oppressed by a secret."

Angela gave a nervous laugh. "I don't know what you mean."

"I mean a secret too big for you, one that weighs you down."

She flushed again, then caught herself. "It isn't your business."

"Not unless it's connected to Lindsay Urson. Then it's my business."

"It's not anything to do with her. It's not possible," Angela said, but she jumped up from her chair. "I've got to go now. I've got to get back before homeroom at the end of the day."

"Wait a sec," I said. I took out one of my business cards and scribbled the Seafarer's Inn phone number. "Just in case you think of something. Or change your mind."

"No," she said.

"Please. You never know." She hesitated a moment, then pocketed the card. "Thanks for lunch."

"My pleasure," I said.

I signaled for the bill, paid quickly, and stepped out onto the street in time to see her disappear into the small mall where I had been window shopping. I went into the hardware store next door and pretended an interest in a display of bird feeders and snow shovels. A couple of moments later, Angela reappeared with a tall, blond man who was carrying a large, unwieldy box. As they headed quickly down the street, the man glanced back over his shoulder, and I recognized Peter Laurimer, the Madrigal Society director. He should have been in school, too, although Esther Reed had said his job was only part time.

I left the hardware store and walked as fast as I dared after them. There were quite a few shoppers going in and out of the stores, and I tried to keep far enough back so that even if they noticed me, they might think it a coincidence. As they hurried past the cheese shop, the bookstore, the dress shops, pet store, and jewelry shops, they seemed engrossed in conversation. I followed them into the municipal parking lot in time to see Angela get into a small, dark Ford with Peter Laurimer at the wheel. Perfectly innocent? Possibly. He was the Madrigal Society's director and her voice teacher; perhaps he'd agreed to give her a ride back to school. But somehow I didn't think so.

I was beginning to get the idea that Peter Laurimer was part of what was so obviously weighing on Angela's mind. I remembered his soft, youthful face, and Esther's curious comment that he had a seventeenth-century soul. Rake or Puritan, I wondered, and I thought I'd better find out which.

After an abortive attempt to see Lindsay's gymnastics friend, Patsy Culver, I returned to the Seafarer's Inn and called Esther. My pretext was the purchase of a ticket to the Madrigal Society concert, and I arranged to stop and pick one up from her.

"It should be a good program," she said. "And there's always a nice reception afterwards."

"I'll look forward to that," I said. "Tomorrow at two o'clock?"

"That would be nice," she said. "Try and stay for a cup of tea."

I promised that I would and hung up, hoping that the intelligent and, I guessed, well-informed Esther Reed would be in a chatty mood.

THAT NIGHT I went to the Valons' for dinner with the family, an ordeal half social and half professional. Much as I liked Alex, I found Dottie too managerial, too nosy, and altogether too vivacious. She was a joy, however, compared to her daughter Cynthia, a tall, quite striking woman with an aggrieved and disapproving air. Neighborhood gossip suggested that she had her reasons, but I began to suspect she'd given as good as she'd got. She was not a soothing personality, and it was soon clear that the Valon household had split into a variety of semi-hostile factions.

Scott and his grandfather were united against the women, who found fault with both. Cynthia kept up a stream of directions and reproofs that her son largely ignored, while Dottie directed a similar, if more tactful, flow at Cynthia. Alex retreated into Scott's company, or, since I was there, into reminiscence, while Dottie amused herself by constantly asking for amplification of purposely vague statements. I couldn't help thinking of peaceful dinners with Harry and wondering, in an unserious sort of way, how much children would have changed us. I'd been non-maternal from day one, but Harry might have made a good father, providing someone was around to keep the darlings out of his workshop.

I was considering that and nodding at the right times to a recital of neighborhood gossip when the phone rang. Alex took it in the foyer and as we heard him say, "No, she's not here," I had an unpleasant memory of Sidonie Urson's late-night call. "I'll ask," Alex said. "Wait just a minute." He stuck his head around the door and said, "Scott, did you see Angela today?"

"Just at school this morning."

"Not later? That's her mother."

Scott shook his head. "She wasn't on the bus this afternoon," he said.

"No," Alex said. "Scott says he didn't see her this afternoon." There was a pause. "Oh, I see. Well, she can't have gotten very far in that time." Another pause. "Yes, she's here. Just a minute." Alex returned. "That's Isabel Browning. Angela got back this afternoon early, went out, and hasn't come back."

"I saw her this noon," I said, "but certainly not since."

"Maybe you could talk to her," Alex said.

I got up and went into the foyer. "Isabel, Anna Peters."

"You saw Angela today," she began, her voice in the accusatory mode.

"I took her to lunch. It seems that she was off early for Founders' Day."

"Angela cut school," Isabel said furiously. "I'd have appreciated a call."

"I'm not the truant officer," I said. "And as a matter of fact, I haven't been able to reach you folks."

"I don't want you talking to Angela. She's just about over this whole nightmare, and you start stirring things up again."

"Angela was already in the center when I saw her. And I'm not sure I'd characterize her as having gotten ten over anything. There's something—"

But before I could continue, Isabel cut me off. "Angela's gone! She just left the house without a word to anyone."

"She got a ride from Peter Laurimer this afternoon. Have you called him?"

There was an awkward silence at the other end. Then Isabel said, "I'm sure she's with some of her friends."

"Where do the kids go? Some mall? The center?"

"I'm sure she'll be somewhere in the Estates," Isabel said.

"Well, good luck," I said, and hung up. Dottie entertained us for a time with speculations about Angela in particular and the Brownings in general, and I left early. The next morning, Alex phoned me to say that Angela had been picked up in the neighboring mall around midnight.

"Disoriented," Alex said. "That was Tosh's word."

"That's a young lady with a lot of troubles."

"I'm beginning to think so. Just a word, Anna. I'd avoid the Brownings. They're rather blaming you for this."

"I thought that was going to be the line last night. See if you can find out anything more from Chief Stoughton, all right?"

"Yes, but I'm not sure it's relevant."

"Angela knows something. She as much as told me that at lunch yesterday. I think she'd like to tell me, but I'm getting the distinct feeling that her parents would rather she didn't. I'd like to know why."

"If that's the case," Alex said thoughtfully, "I'd like to know why, too."

ELEVEN

IT WAS SUNNY, even warm, in the yard at the Seafarer's Inn, and I decided to look up William Brighton before I visited Esther Reed. The photography store was only a few shops down from where I'd met Angela, and its location suggested that she might have been hurrying to see William as easily as Peter Laurimer. When the clerk told me that Brighton was not expected in that day, I went back to my car and drove down Wharf Street, then along the marshes, past Esther Reed's cottage and some brackish ponds, to the river.

The marina Bradley had mentioned was half a mile farther, squeezed between the road and the water. It consisted of an old, blackened shingle barn, a modern control booth, and a long stretch of wharf that once must have docked fishing boats, whalers and packet steamers but now held an assortment of sailboats and power craft. There was a rough parking lot next to the barn and, on the edge, several small gray sheds.

The wind surprised me when I got out of my car. It came careening in off the Sound with breath-catching bursts and, in between times, blew hard enough to make my eyes water. Three miles away it was Indian summer; the shore had skipped a couple months and settled into November. The dock was, with reason, deserted, and I guessed that the prudent management

of The River Marina Company was holed up inside
somewhere. I walked back through the parking lot and
over to the sheds. The first two were small with pad-
locked doors and cobwebbed windows, revealing old
lobster traps, sails, rope, planks, and mysterious bits
and pieces of marine regalia. The third was larger, a
two-story affair with a conventional door and a bas-
ket for mail. A large, powerful-looking motorcycle
was chained to a block of concrete. I knocked on the
door, then called, but the building was only a few feet
from the water and the strong, steady wind whipped
my words away. I tried the door, found it unlocked,
and stepped inside.

After the brilliant glare of the sun on the water, the
interior seemed very dark and it took my eyes a moment to adjust. There was a counter on one side with
a phone and a chair—the watchman's post. The rest
of the lower floor seemed to be used for storage, for
there was the same clutter of maritime implements as
in the other sheds and a powerful smell of dust, salt,
and wood. Strong gusts rattled the windows and,
without the sunlight, it felt even colder inside than out.
If William Brighton was playing the rebel and outcast, he was certainly doing it right.

"William! Brighton!" I thought I heard someone
move above and looked about for the stairs. I found
them behind a partition at the back, looking old,
steep, and narrow. The place seemed empty, but the
door to the apartment above was closed and, after a
final shout, I went up and knocked. When there was
no answer, I tried the handle.

"William?" I stepped into a dark and moldy-
smelling anteroom. Beyond, I could see windows with

white sea light seeping in around the drawn blinds, an unmade bed, another door. I did not get time to see anything else, because the shadows rose up beside me and struck me hard across the shoulder and the side of my head. The phrase "clubbed to death" exploded in my mind, and I dropped to the floor, rolled over and kicked out with both legs as hard as I could. Someone gave a cry of surprise, then a lot of blond hair tumbled into view, a beard and long, strong hands clutching a stick. I grabbed for one end, and William, half dressed and white with fear, jerked me painfully across the floor. We were struggling over what I realized was a kitchen broom handle when I found breath enough to gasp, "It's Anna Peters. I met you at my husband's show. At the gallery."

He stopped trying to tear the handle from my grasp and looked at me. His eyes were dark and enormous, and I saw that my first impression had been correct: He was terrified. I released my grip and sat up. "It's all right," I said. "I didn't mean to frighten you. I'm Anna Peters. I met you last spring."

He nodded.

"I called from downstairs. Didn't you hear me? The wind is so strong, I—"

"I heard you," he said, sitting back on his heels. I was uncomfortably aware that if I were wrong about him, I wasn't in the best of positions. The marina was deserted, and, though skinny, William was surely a good deal heavier and stronger than I. I'm getting too old for this, I thought, and a muscle in my lower back concurred.

"I wanted to talk to you," I said as slowly and calmly as possible. "The photography shop said you were only in evenings. I had to be in the area, so I thought I'd stop in."

He nodded without speaking.

"Bradley Urson had mentioned you were the caretaker here. When no one was around outside, I tried the door."

William got to his feet, and I made myself get up slowly, too.

"Your face is bleeding," he said. His voice was perfectly neutral, as if his emotions were kept a long way away.

I put my hand up and felt blood above my left eye. The broom handle had caught my eyebrow and sliced it open like a boxer's jab.

"I'm glad you didn't have anything bigger," I said. "Do you have a paper towel or something?" The blood was beginning to run into my eye.

"Yeah, through there in the darkroom." There was again the funny separation between idea and action, before William went through the main room, opened a door, and produced a wad of paper towels.

"Thanks." There was a mirror on one wall and I went over and inspected the damage.

"I didn't mean to hurt you," he mumbled.

"No major damage," I said, although I could now feel a bruise on one hip; my shoulder didn't feel right either. I'd pay for all this foolishness tomorrow. "You might think of a different greeting for visitors."

"I was asleep," he said. "I do my developing after work at the store. I was there late last night."

It passed through my mind that he was lucky Angela had been found. "Funny how startled you can be if you're waked up unexpectedly," I said. Then I turned away from the mirror and looked at him. "Or were you expecting someone else?"

William's face was blankly indifferent. From the first time I began to think Bradley was right: Under his disconnected and wounded air, William might be pretty tough.

"I came to see you because you were in or about the Ursons' garage the night of the murder. I wondered if you'd seen anybody."

"The police have already asked that."

"Not everyone is candid with the police."

William gave a snorting sound that might have passed for a laugh.

"There's something else," I said. "There's Angela."

"What about Angela?" he asked quickly.

"She was missing for a time last night. She cut school, too. Do you know anything about that?"

"She didn't come to see me, if that's what you're thinking. I haven't seen Angela in a long time."

"I talked to Angela just yesterday."

"Yeah?"

"She mentioned she saw you around."

"Oh, yeah, in the center. But just to talk to. I mean, we don't go out or anything."

I believed him. He seemed too gauche for Angela, who, at barely fourteen, aspired to sophistication. "Angela is afraid," I said.

William shrugged.

"Angela is very much afraid of something—of someone."

"Not me," he said with quick defensiveness.

"Of someone in town, though. That's my guess. She's afraid of someone who lives around here."

William looked uncomfortable.

"You like Angela, don't you?"

"Yeah, sure. She's real nice."

"You wouldn't want to see anything happen to her?"

"Listen," William said, "none of this has anything to do with me, you know. I mean, I'm sorry, but it's nothing to do with me."

"Unless you know something. Unless you saw something the night Lindsay Urson was killed."

"Everyone thinks I did it. So then, you know, I must have seen something."

"If you did it, yes." I watched his eyes; the fear had gone. William was alert to his emotions, I saw, as if he wanted to catch himself before he felt anything.

"Everyone believes that," he said almost hopefully. He'd been despised; now he was feared. I saw he preferred fear and wondered what that preference would do to him.

"Some people see Scott Cushing as the one."

"Scott's a jerk."

"Jerks have been murderers."

"Naw, not Scott."

"You sound very sure."

"I know Scott. He's just an asshole. He breaks windows and steals bicycles, that kind of crap. He thought Lindsay was a dope. This was a beautiful girl and he says, 'She's so boring,' know what I mean?"

I knew. "My thought was that you'd seen someone else while you were putting the car away or were sitting smoking in it. Maybe you were waiting for someone."

"Who the hell would that be?"

"I don't know. Maybe Lindsay."

"Don't give me that shit!" His voice was dangerous.

"All right, not Lindsay. But you saw someone, someone you haven't mentioned to the police. And Angela knows, too."

"No, that's all crap."

"Angela is frightened. Angela is frightened for herself. And you were terrified when I came up the stairs."

"I told you," he said, his voice rising, "I told you I was fucking asleep."

"With your door unlocked? Thank God you didn't have a two-by-four or a baseball bat handy—or a golf club. You couldn't have escaped a second charge."

"Why the hell should I care?" he asked. "What the hell am I going to be able to do anyway? Take pictures of some creep's fucking boat? That's what I can do. I can't leave here. I tried, you know. I tried a couple jobs over in New Haven, down in the city. What happens. Cops call up, 'Mr. Brighton is under investigation in the Urson murder case—just for your information.' Do you think I can get a job? I'll be stuck at this stupid marina 'til I'm sixty."

"You could be spending time with the feds. I don't think you'd like that nearly as much."

He turned away and began pounding his hands one into the other.

"If you did kill her, you're lucky. If you didn't, you ought to see about clearing yourself."

"How the hell do I do that?"

"Hire investigators, get another lawyer."

"I don't have any money. Get that through your head. I'm broke!"

"Borrow from your parents. Take out a loan."

"I can't," he said. "No one will—"

"Or stop feeling sorry for yourself and tell me what you do know."

"That's it, isn't it? Everyone wants to know what I know."

"Who else?" I asked.

"You don't need to know. You're acting for that jerk Scott. They want to blame me, you know that. The Valons, that bitch Cushing—it's not going to work. I'll get out of here."

"Suit yourself." I scribbled my phone number on one of my cards and handed it over. "If you change your mind."

William glanced at it and dropped it on the floor. "Good-bye," he said. "You woke me up. I'm going back to bed." He stretched and turned back toward his bed.

"Just one thing," I said.

William stopped without looking around.

"What are you getting out of this? Out of being a suspect?"

William turned around and came over until he was quite close to me, too close, to tell the truth. "Now I don't get hassled. Now I don't have to put up with being hassled." He put his hand on my arm and I thought it best to stay still and calm. There was a lot of anger under his wounded eyes and vacant expression. "See," he said, as if he could read my mind.

"Even you're wondering, aren't you? So don't come back, you understand that? Don't come back again."

I PULLED UP AT Esther Reed's house just a little before two. I got out and stood by the car in the warm sunshine for a minute, trying to convince the rear portions of my anatomy that standing, sitting, and walking were going to continue to be good ideas. Among our many services to what we like to refer to as "the security-conscious portions of our business community" have been a series of workshops on self-defense techniques. My personal knowledge is considerable but largely theoretical; maybe Sue Tansi was right about the need for appropriate exercise.

I rubbed my shoulder, then checked my face in the mirror. I'd had to forgo the paper towel to drive to Esther's, and a fat new trickle of blood was adding to what was liberally smeared along the side of my face. I was just getting the worst removed and wishing I had some sort of bandage when a car pulled in behind me. Dressed in a pair of brown coveralls, Esther Reed got out and waved as the driver pulled away.

"Sorry I'm late. I had a flight at the last minute. Did you see my message?"

"I haven't quite gotten there yet."

"You need a Band-Aid," she said.

"Maybe more than one."

She raised her eyebrows and walked over to the door. There was a note scrawled in large and emphatic handwriting.

"I didn't realize you were a pilot."

"I may be the only middle-aged, female, lute-playing pilot in Connecticut," she said.

We both laughed, and I reminded myself to assume nothing.

"I'll get some antiseptic."

"I think it's clean."

"Nonetheless." She came back with a bottle, some cotton wool, and a box of bandages. I'd found the sink and had most of the blood washed off.

"Not very big but still bleeding," she said.

"Facial cuts are the worst. Ouch."

"This stuff's very strong. No chance of infection with it."

I felt as though someone had rubbed my eyes with jalapeño peppers. "I'm glad to hear it."

"I think one large bandage will do, but you'd better take a couple extras."

"Thanks. I didn't lay in a first-aid kit."

"It's clear you weren't a girl scout."

"Just one of those silly accidents."

Esther Reed smiled noncommittally and said she'd be changed in a minute. I was delegated to start the tea, and after I'd put on the kettle, I looked around the kitchen. It was extremely neat and extremely tiny: very like an airplane cockpit, in fact, with a lot of drawers and cupboards and built-in appliances. There was one stretch of wall that held several photographs and drawings of small planes. I recognized a much younger Esther beside a rather stout, white-haired man.

"My father," Esther said. She had changed into a good pleated tartan skirt and a sweater. "He designed aircraft."

"And this is you, too?"

"The day I got my commercial pilot's license."

"And that's what you do now?"

"That and teach. I like having my own hours and having time for music. With the number of company headquarters and CEOs here, there's no lack of work. And you?"

"I tend to earthbound executives. This visit is something of a sideline. A favor to Alex Valon."

"I see. The business with Scott?"

"Yes, the Urson case."

"Was that why you wanted to see me?"

"Well, that and the ticket. I really enjoy music."

"But this is partly business?"

"Partly. The Madrigal Society is partly business."

"In what way?" She filled the teapot and set it on a tray beside a plate of cookies.

"I'm not sure. Mostly, I want to know a little more about Angela."

"Surely Angela is not under suspicion."

"No, no, although only Martha is her alibi. But it's not that."

When I hesitated, Esther said, "I know how to be discreet."

"I'm relying on that. A couple of things bother me. First, Angela was terrified when Lindsay was killed. And she's still very frightened."

"A lot of people were frightened," Esther said reasonably. "It was a very frightening thing."

"With Angela it went a bit deeper," I said. "She also felt guilty about leaving Lindsay alone."

Esther raised her eyebrows slightly.

"I know, that sounds natural, too. But the other thing is that all my conversations about the case come back to Angela. Lindsay was the kid nobody knew; Angela was the one people talk about. Everyone agrees she's precocious, maybe reckless. I'd like to know about her friends, about her life. It seems a bit oblique, I'm sure, but I've gotten more and more convinced that the way to find out about Lindsay is through Angela."

"And the way to Angela is through the Madrigal Society?"

"Maybe. I'm thinking maybe through Peter Laurimer."

"No, I don't think—" she stopped and took a deep breath. "This is between you and me."

"Of course. Along with the rest of the conversation, I hope."

"Peter is a man surprisingly attractive to women. To a certain kind of woman, anyway. Look at Miriam, now."

"Miriam, the alto?"

"Yes. Miriam Greene. She has a perfectly good husband. Marvin's better-looking than Peter any day of the week and he makes millions. Literally. He runs a chain of shoe stores. Do you know she lost—it must have been twenty-five or thirty pounds for him."

"For Marvin?"

"Oh no, Peter. All last year she was dieting—she'd bring carrot and celery sticks to rehearsal as her share of the snacks. I asked her why one day and she said she was 'getting into fighting trim.' And she has."

"She's certainly good looking. I saw her at the service."

"She was a professional model. Still works occasionally—that's why the gloves."

"Gloves?"

"Surely you saw her while you were staying with the Brownings? She doesn't even walk the dogs without gloves."

"Does she live near the Estates?"

"She's the Valons' neighbor."

She must have seen my confusion, because she added, "They have the house behind Alex and Dottie's."

"Dottie told me the Ems lived there. I'd gotten a map—"

"That's right. The M's—Miriam and Marvin. We've called them that for years—sort of a joke."

I thought it might become a bad one. "You said she always wears gloves?"

"She was a hand model—you know, those perfect hands holding the all-important product? Never a flaw, never a cracked nail or a scratch. Ask her, she'll tell you all about it. Creams at night, never washes dishes without rubber gloves, never does anything manual, wears gloves whenever she's outside. I guess it's habit now, but her hands are quite amazing. They could belong to a girl of seventeen." Esther looked at her own tanned and lined hands ruefully.

"So hands and all, she set her sights on Peter Laurimer?"

"And brought up the heavy artillery." Esther laughed. "But don't take that too seriously. Miriam's what we used to call a flirt."

"I remember the term."

"From several thousand years ago—like me. Anyway, she craves attention; she has to be the femme fatale. I'm not sure it goes much further than that. At least most of the time. She and Marvin seem to get along pretty well on the whole."

"I hear a lot of qualifications and reservations."

"I'm not much of a gossip," Esther said.

"Normally a virtue, but in this case, I'm not so sure. There's something odd here. Even Miriam's habits might be important."

"You're worried, aren't you?"

"Yes. About Angela, mostly. I'm not much of a gossip either, but maybe you should know she went missing last night. Only temporarily, but she wound up at the shopping mall. 'Disoriented' was the word."

"Drugs, you mean?"

"No one's saying. I think emotionally disoriented, myself. She told me earlier in the day that she thought she might lose her voice. How does that happen to singers?"

"Damage to the vocal cords, infection, smoking sometimes . . ."

"I think we can rule those out."

"Sometimes it's emotional. Loss of nerve."

"I thought something like that. Another thing—she and Miriam don't get along, do they?"

"Miriam was used to being the absolute center of attention. The gorgeous woman with the gorgeous voice. Although a tremendous artistic addition, Angela has presented certain problems."

"The heir apparent?"

"Something like that."

"This rivalry—just for Laurimer's attention, do you think?"

"Who else?"

"William, maybe."

Esther laughed and said, "I wouldn't think so."

"Don't be too quick. He knows Angela and likes her. He lived at the Gores', which means he must know Miriam. He is very good looking."

"Not Miriam's type."

"No?"

"Power, importance, a suitable setting for her glamor—that's what Miriam wants from a man."

"I see. Nothing so tasteless as youth and beauty. Well, who else might she and Angela know? What about Ken Browning?"

Esther looked serious. "There was some talk," she said after a pause. "There was some talk about Ken and Miriam. But, to be fair, there's always talk about him."

"Another reason for Angela to dislike her."

"Oh yes, I think that's true. But basically I think it's been competition. For Ms. Golden Voice of Branch Hill."

I was tapping my fingers on my cup.

"You're not satisfied with that?" Esther asked.

"I'm still thinking about William. Do you know how he supports himself?"

"He works part time at the photography shop and I understand he is caretaker at the old marina now."

"That seems barely enough to live on, yet he has a new motorcycle. I just was wondering."

"His parents are very wealthy."

"No, I don't think that's the source. William's rather enjoying his outlaw image at the moment."

"He seems to have impressed you," Esther said dryly.

"It was one of those situations," I said, touching the Band-Aid.

"He attacked you?"

"With a broom handle—only thing he had handy, fortunately."

"Did you report that? The police should know. I'd heard he's supposed to have a violent temper, but I didn't know..."

"This wasn't temper," I said. "He was scared to death. Like Angela. That's what bothers me. That and the fact that his door was unlocked."

"What do you mean?"

"I mean that he was waiting for someone, and if he heard me call, it must have been a woman."

TWELVE

IT WAS ONE OF Esther Reed's eccentricities that she refused to own a car, and I offered to drop her at the Madrigal Society rehearsal.

"Do I detect an ulterior motive?" she asked.

"I thought I might come in for just a moment. I'd like to see if Angela is all right, for one thing."

"We'll be in trouble for next week if she isn't," Esther said as she put her sheet music into a leather portfolio. "I don't think Mindy Johnson is ready for solo work."

"How does Angela get to rehearsals from school?"

"I believe she takes the school bus that comes through the center on rehearsal days. Or Isabel brings her. She used to ride home with Miriam, but I notice she hasn't done that for some time. Miriam offers, but Angela always makes some excuse."

The Madrigal Society had the use of one of the rooms in the parish hall of St. George's. Esther and I arrived early so that she could fetch the key for a square, drab room with the well worn floor and chipped woodwork of its ilk. A red and gold painted harpsichord was concealed under a brown cotton cover and a metal locker held an assortment of music stands.

I was helping her set them up when Peter Laurimer arrived. He looked both younger and more harried than I had remembered, a tall, thin-faced man with a lock of fair hair tumbling into his eyes. He had a black sweater on over his shirt and tie, like the poets of my youth, and he gave the impression of being not so much nervous as intense and tightly strung. He didn't remember me and when Esther said that I was a friend of the Valons and the Brownings, he only nodded and began fussing with the music. He was sorting some photocopied sheets when Miriam Greene arrived, looking stylish in a navy silk shirtdress with a white satin ascot, followed by some of the other singers, including Angela.

Miriam made directly for Peter and began discussing some detail of a Dowland piece they were to sing. I asked Angela if she was feeling better.

"Oh, much. Everything's fine. Parents panic."

"But not you?"

She gave me a sly look and went over to the harpsichord. "We'd better be good today. Anna notices everything."

Peter Laurimer seemed puzzled.

"Miriam knows, don't you Miriam? That Anna's a famous private investigator. And she's talking to absolutely everyone, aren't you, Anna?"

"I'm not sure I did know that," Miriam said. Really, she was born too late. Despite her slim and, admittedly, youthful elegance, she had a dowager's air.

"Oh, yes." Like a much younger child, Angela seemed anxious to stir up friction. "She saw me yesterday. My folks were furious," adding to me, "I don't think you'll be invited again."

I ignored this. "I saw a friend of yours, too. William Brighton."

"William is a nasty little sneak," Miriam said.

Angela laughed. "Miriam doesn't like artists."

"Artists! He's the next thing to a Peeping Tom. How he wasn't arrested just amazes me."

"Arrested for what?" I asked.

"Nothing. William takes pictures," Angela said. "He's making a portrait of Branch Hill and all its depravity." She looked at Miriam and laughed.

"He's the sort who hides in bushes," Miriam said, "and takes silly candids all over town."

"Really?"

"I make it my business to know what goes on in Branch Hill. William Brighton doesn't belong here at all and the sooner he's encouraged to move on, the better."

"I should think the police would just as soon he stay where they can keep an eye on him," I said.

"They'd have done better to arrest him. They could have found evidence."

"William's completely harmless," Angela said. "There was nothing against him."

"Except being out wandering about the night your friend was murdered. I'm surprised at you, Angela. Not very surprised, but a little surprised."

"Perhaps we could begin," Laurimer said impatiently. I'd noticed that the gossip and sparring were making him increasingly restless and annoyed.

The others began to assemble their music and adjust their stands, but Angela said, "Maybe he had his camera with him. How about that, Miriam? Maybe he did."

"Angela, are you ready? This is going to take a lot of work." Laurimer's voice was sharp. I had thought

him ineffectual, but once installed at the harpsichord, his demeanor changed.

Angela put her chin in the air. "I'm just getting my
music. I don't know if I'm going to manage to sing
much today anyway."

"Too many late nights," Miriam said under her
breath.

"That's not true," Angela said. "I haven't felt
well."

Laurimer did not allow himself to be drawn into
their bickering. Now he was all business, the odd intensity of his nature focused. He gave them their notes
from the harpsichord, then stood up and tapped on
one of the metal stands. A silent expectancy descended. "Let's start with 'Sweet, do not destroy me
with flying.' Esther, if you'd give us the intro. We'll try
this tempo first." As he began humming the melody
and beating the time with one hand, I waved to Esther and left. I was on the steps down to the main
hallway when the voices joined the melancholy notes
of the lute. They rose strong and clear, but Laurimer
stopped them almost immediately. "You're not the
Yale Glee Club," I heard him say. "Don't bellow. Remember, he had the soul of his age, and that soul was
secret, passionate, and glorious. Emphasis, please, on
passion and secrecy. Let's try it again. From the
top..."

It was close to four-thirty, and I decided that it
wouldn't hurt to see if Patsy Culver had showed up at
the gymnastics center. When I arrived, the parking lot
was jammed with station wagons, minivans, big se-
dans, and flocks of small girls with huge, pastel colored backpacks and gym bags. I recognized Tansi's

assistant and, with her help, located Patsy Culver. She was tiny, half Lindsay's size, with perfectly cut short chestnut hair, a snub nose, and a great many freckles. Her pink leotard looked child-sized and her face and figure so immature that her deep, rather grown-up voice came as a surprise.

"Of course, I knew Lindsay well. We've been—we were—on the team together for four years." She scanned the new arrivals as if searching for Lindsay in the arriving crowd. "I still can't believe it, you know."

"I wondered if I might ask you some questions."

"The police asked me a lot of questions," Patsy said earnestly. "I told them everything I could remember."

"I have a couple of specific questions. Did Lindsay have a boyfriend?"

"Oh, they asked me that. No. She kinda liked Scott Cushing, but he's goofy. And anyway, that's just because he lived near her and she felt she knew him."

"No one else? No one older, maybe?"

"Lindsay was awfully shy. Nobody knew that. I mean, she always looked so wonderful, but she was shy. I think that makes boys shy, too, don't you?"

"Yes, I'm sure you're right."

Her eyes wandered to the other girls assembling in the gym.

"There's only one thing more," I said. "Ms. Tansi mentioned that someone came to see Lindsay a day or so before she was killed. A woman, tall, in a dark dress with sunglasses. Do you remember that?"

Patsy fidgeted and shrugged. "It's hard to remember. It's months ago now."

"Ms. Tansi said Lindsay had been—upset or annoyed. She said she was only away from the gym for a minute."

"Mrs. Greene came by one day. Boy, was Lindsay pissed about that!"

"Mrs. Greene? Miriam Greene, her neighbor?"

"Yeah."

"Why was Lindsay annoyed about that?"

"William—do you know William?"

"William Brighton?"

"Yeah. He'd told Mrs. Greene that Lindsay would have some pictures for her. I guess he'd been doing some photography for the Greenes."

"And?"

"He hadn't given Lindsay anything. Anyway, she wouldn't have run an errand for him."

"I see. Why do you think he told Mrs. Greene that?" And why, come to think of it, had Miriam gone all the way downtown, when she could have stopped by the Ursons' house?

"I don't know. Just to annoy her, I guess. William's weird like that. He'll do things or say things just to see how people will react."

"And Mrs. Greene got mad at Lindsay?"

"Yeah. Lindsay said she was yelling and everything. Lindsay turned around and walked away. She pretended she didn't mind, but she didn't like to have anything to do with the guys her dad was helping. She didn't like them at all."

"That's very helpful," I said.

"Is that all? Can I go now?"

I could hear the sound of whistles. "Yes. Thank you very much."

She scooted for the gym, but stopped in the doorway and turned around. "I really liked Lindsay. Not
everyone understood her, but she was really great,"
Patsy said. Then with a funny little wave she disappeared into the organized chaos of gymnastics practice.

I went into the phone booth in the lobby and tried
to contact William first at the marina, then at the
photography store. I did a few errands in town, tried
again to reach him, without success, and had an early
dinner. It was seven when I got back to the Seafarer's
Inn, and, this time, William answered on the second
ring.

"Sorry about what happened this afternoon," he
said when I identified myself. "You're okay, aren't
you?"

I wondered if he were still middle-class enough to
envision suits and claims. "No problem, but I would
like to see you for a few minutes. There's something I
need to ask you about."

There was a silence, as if he were thinking things
over, then he said that I could come over, but not right
away. "I've got some developing to do."

"All right. What's convenient for you?"

"Around nine. Okay?"

"Nine would be fine. Can I meet you somewhere in
the center?"

"No," he said. "I've got too much work to do.
Come to my place," and he hung up.

I called Harry, compared notes on home decora-
tion with Mrs. Weaver, the inn proprietor, and wasted
some time with a paperback novel. At 8:45, I got into
my car, and, at nine on the dot, I pulled into the ma-

rina parking lot, which looked even colder and emptier at night than it had in the daytime. I had passed only a couple of cars on the way, and except for the lights along the wharf and William's window, the whole area was dark and quiet. After listening to the wind for a moment, I got out of the car and opened the trunk. The rental car came equipped with a set of tools, including a wrench that had a nice, solid feel. Although I couldn't see William as anything more than a troubled—and frightened—adolescent, I slipped the wrench into my purse before I locked the car. Then I knocked on William's door. There was no answer, but when I stepped inside, I heard a stereo playing with a lot of heavy bass. The downstairs lights were on and, taking that as a sign I was expected, I climbed the stairs and thumped on the apartment door. "William? It's Anna Peters."

The stereo played on. I could hear someone with a hoarse voice and a limited vocabulary shouting over the guitars.

"William!" Disinclined to be pounced on again by that overgrown and nervous adolescent, I gave the door a good kick, and the knob, loose on my previous visit, rattled onto the floor. I picked it up in exasperation and refitted it on the spindle, tripping the latch in the process. "It's Anna," I shouted as the door opened. "Anna Peters."

There was no answer, only the piledriver bass and the thin whinny of a guitar, but all the lights were on, and I stepped inside. There were papers on the bed, I saw that first, and lots of black-and-white photographs strewn about like dirty snow. There was some red, too, spotted on the bed and on the floor beside the chunky leather motorcycle boots that seemed too heavy and clumsy for the long, thin legs protruding from them. William lay sprawled on the floor with his head against a corner of the cast iron stove that heated the place. There was a lot of blood on his face and on the back of his head and it was darkening the old, gray, unsealed wood floor.

I caught my breath against shock and the smell of sweat and blood, then forced myself to walk over and put my hand on his chest. As soon as I felt his heartbeat, I jumped up. The phone was beside the bed, half buried under clothes and photographs, and I punched up 911 for an ambulance and the police. Then I turned off the stereo and pulled a blanket off the bed, dislodging another wave of photographs. Without the stereo, I could hear William's hoarse and labored breathing. He'd been in a fight, clearly. I could see that his hands were scraped, but there was so much blood that it was hard to assess the damage, and after I wrapped him in the blanket, I went looking for a towel.

The first door I tried led to the darkroom. The light was on inside and showed pans overturned, strips of film thrown on the floor, another litter of photos. I left that door open and tried the next one. The bathroom was cramped and untidy. I grabbed the nearest towel, wet it, and went back to try to clean William's face. I soon saw that there were no cuts; the blood seemed to be coming from his nose and mouth, a bad sign. His long hair was sticky with blood, too, and I assumed he'd gashed his head when he fell against the stove. Desperate for activity, I mopped up as much as

I could, then ran downstairs and opened the outside door for the emergency people.

Back in the apartment, I listened helplessly to William's breathing. My medical expertise doesn't extend very far, but it was clear that he was seriously injured, and I went to the window to see if there was any sign of the ambulance. As I leaned on the sill, I noticed I'd gotten my hands bloody and, hoping I'd had no cuts or scratches, went to wash.

I was in the bathroom doorway, drying my hands, when I noticed one picture out of all the dozens littering the floor. It was a small print of two young girls with beautiful long hair. They were walking away from the camera but looking back, smiling over their shoulders. They wore long dark dresses; their hair looked thick and fair and from just that angle and in just that light, Angela Browning and Lindsay Urson looked almost identical. It was a charming picture of sunlight and of young girls with fey, delightful smiles, but it gave me a shock, so sudden and intense, that for a moment I didn't recognize the sirens or the shouts and the sounds of running feet on the coarse crushed rock of the parking lot. Then I threw open the inner door and called, "Up here! Bring a stretcher!"

The first medical technician, a heavy black man with close-cut hair and a little square mustache, mounted the stairs two at a time, his bag in hand. I pointed and he pushed past me and knelt down beside William. Two more medics, a man and a woman, followed with a stretcher.

"How long?" the first technician asked.

"I don't know. I just got here—maybe five minutes ago."

He had his stethoscope on William's chest and didn't seem to like what he was hearing. Meanwhile, the other two had loosened the blanket and cut William's shirt so that they could start an IV solution.

"You know him?"

"William Brighton. I think his parents live in Greenwich. The police will know."

I got out of the way as the medical technicians went to work, their leader calling out information as he continued his examination. They had William on the stretcher before the first cops came banging up the narrow stairs.

"Oh, shit," one said. He was big and fair like the police chief, but very young. Now that the medics had moved William, the sinister pool of blood by the stove was clearly visible.

"We gotta take him in right away," the chief medic said. "He'll be lucky to make it."

"You know what happened?" the cop asked me.

"I found him on the floor, place a mess."

The policeman's partner had arrived; they both looked around the room as if this was going to take some time to absorb.

"Careful with the stair," the woman said. She was steadying the IV bottle as the other two maneuvered the stretcher through the door. I saw William tilted up sharply as they descended the steep flight, then the door banged below, and a radio crackled before the siren started up like a lost soul. I heard the police phone calling for assistance and realized that one officer was talking to me.

"Yes?"

"Officer Murphy," he repeated. "Your name?"

I told him, produced my license and an abundance of identification, mentioned his police chief, and said I thought I'd like to sit down: Blood and violence are a shock every time.

"This guy was a photographer?"

"He worked at the shop in town and took pictures on his own. Boats, I'm told."

"There don't seem to be too many boat pictures here."

That was the second officer, Murphy's partner. He had untidy brown hair, a long jaw, and small deep-set eyes like central casting's idea of a hillbilly singer.

"Someone told me he was taking pictures of all of Branch Hill. Those might be the ones."

"Looks like someone was interested in them." He looked at me.

"They were all over the place when I came in. Not so many on the floor. I tipped a lot off getting a blanket for him. I assumed he'd be in shock."

"Touch anything else?" Officer Murphy asked.

"The door, of course, and the phone. I got a towel from the bathroom—and touched the taps. I thought first he was bleeding from a facial cut."

"He was lying against the stove?"

"Yes. He probably fell and hit his head. Or was pushed and hit his head."

They were still examining the floor when reinforcements arrived in the form of Detective Canelli, whom I'd met at the police station. He looked as if he'd been called away from some project in his basement, for he was dressed in a T-shirt and jeans and smelled of paint thinner. We went over all the preliminaries again, and, round about the time the police photographer got to

work, Canelli pulled over the apartment's other
straight chair and sat down beside me.

"So you came to see Brighton?"

"Yes. I'd called him earlier. He said that he had to
go out, but that he could meet me at nine. I was here
right on time."

"When did you call him?"

"I'd tried several times in the afternoon. I finally
got him shortly after seven. I'd say seven-fifteen, no
later."

"What did you want to see him about?"

"Pictures. I'd learned he took a lot of candid pictures of the townspeople, including some Miriam
Greene wanted. I thought I'd ask about that."

"About Miriam Greene or pictures in general?"

"Both. I was curious how he was making ends meet.
That nice motorcycle downstairs is worth a lot of
money."

Canelli's mild eyes kept returning to the bandage on
my forehead. "You cut yourself?"

"I got hit with a broom handle last time I came to
see William. He has a tendency to panic. That's why I
called ahead this time."

Canelli studied me, trying to figure how likely it
would have been for me to have clobbered William and
cleaned myself up before calling the police. Age has
certain advantages, and by the time his partner Burt
Wilson had arrived, we'd covered most of the tricky
ground and they'd decided I was harmless, if dubi-
ous.

"We'll want a signed statement."

"Will tomorrow do?"

"Call first," Canelli said. Wilson, who was standing near the bed, asked, "You touch any of these?"

"Just when I took the blanket off. I wanted to keep him warm—"

"Good idea," said Wilson. "Just checking."

I was in the car and halfway to the Seafarer's Inn when I remembered the photo of the two girls, which I'd stuck in my pocket. As soon as I got back to my room, I set the picture on the bureau and looked at it again. William undeniably had talent. But the reason for my interest was different. That lovely photo gave me a motive for Lindsay Urson's murder.

THIRTEEN

THE BAD THING about love is the ruthlessness it engenders. Alex Valon phoned me at nine-fifteen to ask if I'd seen the paper. I had, in fact. The Seafarer's Inn provided a morning paper with each breakfast, and while Mr. Fujimoto, the visiting electronics expert, perused the financial section, I'd zipped past the headlines to the crime news. William had rated two paragraphs, a sign that the reporters had been pressed for time and short of information. He was mentioned as a "figure in the Urson murder inquiries," a nice way of putting "prime suspect," and his condition was described as serious. I knew a bit more because I had just gotten off the phone with the hospital and Lieutenant Canelli: William was on life support with serious head injuries.

"It's terrible, of course," Alex was saying. "But I'm thinking of Scott. This has just got to clear him."

"Well, I don't know about that, Alex," I said. "Brighton was a troubled kid. Logically, there's no reason why his injury and the Urson killing have to be connected."

"This is Branch Hill," Alex said almost jovially. "We're not well stocked with violent criminals. It's been between Scott and William. This clinches it."

It seemed to me that William was to be condemned for having the bad taste to get beaten up. "It's not the first time he'd been in a fight," I said, but Alex wasn't listening.

"If it was William, someone had a good motive for hurting him; if it wasn't, we've got a third person who's to blame for both."

"I can see it from the public relations point of view, but..."

"...all last night," Alex said.

"Excuse me, Alex. A bad line."

"I said, Scott was with me all last night. And Dottie and Cynthia and a couple of her friends."

"Yes, that's good. But you realize there's absolutely no proof..."

"I don't think there's ever going to be proof. Something would have turned up before now if there had been. And listen, Anna, in this town, appearance, not proof, is the key. People just want to know who's credible, who's reliable."

I could see that people who get beaten half to death are somehow uncomfortable.

"But really I'm grateful," Alex continued. "I don't think there's any more for you to do at this end now."

"I found William," I said. His image was still vivid, as was the memory of saying to Miriam, "I saw a friend of yours, too. William Brighton," and of her venomous response; I wondered to what extent I was to blame.

"Oh. I am sorry, Anna."

"I'm afraid I may have stirred up more trouble than we intended."

"It had to come," said Alex. "Tosh kept saying there would be a break. I'm just thankful it came before Scott's chances were ruined. I'm going to start

calling boarding schools this morning. I can't tell you
what a relief this is."

"I'm glad for Scott," I said.

"Just send 'round the bill when it's convenient,
Anna, and call me before you go."

I said I would, but after I hung up, I decided that
the accounting could wait. Alex was satisfied, but the
assumption of William Brighton's culpability was ir-
rational. I checked the street address of Bradley Urson's bank, grabbed my jacket, and went out to the
car. This time I didn't bother with appointments and
phoning ahead. I asked for his office and sent in my
card. On the back, I wrote: "I found William." Bradley came out in five minutes, looking like death, and
shook my hand without speaking. "Hold my calls,
please, Thelma," he told his secretary as he opened the
office door for me.

I stepped into a big room with institutional vinyl
wallpaper and a great many framed pictures of youth
teams and boys-club groups on the walls. Bradley sat
down at his desk and twisted his large, white, well-
cared-for hands. The nails were perfect, but the
knuckles looked red and tender, and the backs of his
hands had a few nicks and scrapes. I found that dis-
quieting, even though I know home improvements can
play havoc with your hands.

"You found William?" he asked. His voice was
hoarse, almost unrecognizable.

"Yes, I'd gone to see him. Twice, in fact." The cut
on my forehead was now a thin, red line, and I
touched it without thinking.

"I called the hospital this morning," Bradley said.
"After I'd read the paper. They said intensive care."

"It's very bad," I said. "He'd been in a fight and beaten up, but the real damage was from a fall, I think. It looked as if he'd hit his head on the woodstove."

Bradley shook his head. "Why?" he asked. "Why would anyone do that?"

"He was a suspect in—"

"I never believed that!" Bradley said before I could finish. "I didn't believe it. Sidonie—I don't know what she believed. You know we're getting divorced?"

I nodded.

"It's not uncommon after a family tragedy. You'd think it would be the other way around, wouldn't you?"

"We have a lot of myths about families," I said.

"About families, about friendship, about love. I suppose they make life bearable."

He spoke with quiet but intense bitterness, and I said, "I'm sorry about William. There was nothing I could do but call for help."

"There wasn't much anyone could do for William."

"There were a lot of photographs in the room. Pictures of people, mostly. I really didn't have much time to look through them. Do you know anything about that?"

"I told you before, he worked as a photographer."

"I'm not being clear. I had a late night. I meant there were pictures strewn all around. The darkroom had been turned upside down, too, as if someone had wanted to find something fast."

Bradley shrugged and seemed uncomfortable but said nothing. I waited a bit, then said, "I noticed William had a new motorcycle. A very spiffy-looking Kawasaki. I was wondering how he got the money for it."

Bradley looked up. "Maybe his parents."

"How likely was that?"

"Not very."

"And the job at the photography store was only part time—weekends and three nights a week."

"He got his apartment free."

"But no cash?"

"That was the deal."

"So I was wondering about the photographs. Someone told me William was making a portrait of Branch Hill 'and all its depravity.' I quote."

"I don't see—"

"William was in or about your garage the night Lindsay was murdered. He's been a suspect all along, but there was never any real evidence, as you know. There are only a couple of people who would have beaten him half to death on those grounds, and you're presumably one of them. The police will certainly be in to see you, by the way. Do you have an alibi for last night?"

"Just a goddamn minute!"

"I came to see you as a favor," I said. "Take my visit as a warning."

He tapped nervously on his desk and looked away. "Greg and I were working on the painting."

"What time?"

"He came over after work—say six-thirty. We wrapped it up around ten and had a pizza."

"Go out for it?"

"No, called. Had it delivered."

"You have no worries if Greg corroborates that."

Bradley looked dreadful anyway.

"They're not interested in your private life," I said. "Not if you don't make a big deal out of it."

He gave a sad smile.

"So," I said. "That presumably leaves your wife and daughter. Can we rule them out?"

"Yes," he said without hesitation.

"All right, then. Who else has a motive? Lindsay's killer, who suspects—or knows—that William was a witness, before, during, or after the fact, or someone else, who wanted an incriminating picture. That's my thought, anyway."

"Do you think he'll die?" Bradley asked if he hadn't been listening at all.

"I don't know. He's on life support. It'll depend. And he may not remember anything about last night even if he's otherwise fine."

"Christ!"

"I want to ask you some questions," I said. "First, could William have been blackmailing someone in Branch Hill?"

"Would he be capable of it, you mean?"

"Yes."

"I think he would. He was so bitter. He was smart, talented, rich, and handsome, so he thought he deserved to be happy. Or at least to be loved. And if he weren't—well, then he'd be an outlaw. William has a very melodramatic approach to life."

"What about your neighbors? Are there any who have the sort of messy private lives that shouldn't see the light of day?"

Bradley sighed. "I'm sure there were a few."

"Try to think of a few living near you—or the Gores. People William might have seen."

"There was some gossip about Miriam Greene," he said after a long pause. "I had a fatherly talk with William one day about her."

"You'd better be more specific."

"She's considered very attractive, that's all, and she was beginning to take an interest in William that I didn't much like."

I suppose it was that prissy tone that put me off— and had made him unpopular about the Estates. "By interest, you mean a sexual interest?"

"Yes. I'm not sure it went beyond looks and remarks."

"How did William react?"

"As usual. Professions of innocence. I'm not sure it wasn't a mistake to have mentioned the subject. Like a lot of self-centered people, William didn't always pick up on social signals."

"The reason he had so many difficulties?"

"Probably."

"Other people have described Miriam as the neighborhood femme fatale. That fair enough?"

"She and Marvin have what they call an open marriage."

"So what's Marvin like?"

"A big, handsome man. Very rich."

"And his personal life?"

Bradley shrugged. "He can afford to do what he pleases."

"With anyone hereabouts?"

"I've never heard that. I've seen him in the city with another woman, but he's the soul of discretion in Branch Hill."

"What about your other friend, Ken Browning?"

"Ken's something of a ladies' man."

"And is Miriam Greene one of the ladies?"

"I heard it was hot and heavy for a time," Bradley said, "at least on his side. I'd guess Marvin knew; I'm not so sure about Isabel. But the rest of us had heard rumors."

"Not the best blackmail material," I said.

Bradley began fooling with his pen. "If William dies, we'll probably never know what happened."

"No. Listen, it's been some time now since the murder. Have you ever come up with a motive for your daughter's death?"

He shook his head. "She was a good kid. No trouble to anyone."

I waited two beats. "And what if it had been Angela?"

He looked startled.

"Angela Browning," I said. "What about if it had been Angela who'd stopped that night at Scott's and Lindsay who had gone straight home?"

"Don't suggest that," he said, his voice rising. "You don't know how many times I've said to myself, why didn't she come home? Why wasn't it someone else?"

"Please, it is important. Try to answer the question." When he said nothing, I took out the photo and handed it over to him. He looked at it, then looked at me, his face sad and curious.

"Where'd you get this?"

"One of William's photos. It suggested something to me. I wondered if it suggested anything to you."

He looked again at the photo, then looked away. "I don't want to think it," he said after a minute. "I don't want to think it was all an accident."

"No one's come up with a reason to harm Lindsay. I just wondered if Angela was a better candidate."

"No," said Bradley abruptly. "She's a child! It's all absurd. It happened, it was a tragedy—I still think someone baffled the security arrangements, got in, got out." He stood up in agitation, leaving me undecided whether he'd come up with nothing or with an idea he didn't want to face.

I got out of my chair and put the photo back in my bag. "Thank you for your time. If you should think of anything, or hear of anything—"

"There isn't anything," Bradley said. "There's nothing at all."

I CALLED Esther Reed from a phone booth outside, one of those minimalist ones that give new meaning to the term "public phone." "How was the rehearsal yesterday?" I asked.

"Long. The Dowland piece is a bear. In fact, we were there so late that a bunch of us went out for dinner."

"Oh? Who went?"

"Well, Angela didn't go; Peter drove her home because she claimed she felt sick. But Miriam went, and

Lyle Briggs, our bass, and Dave Jennings, our second tenor, and Mindy Johnson.''

"You must have been out fairly late.''

"We didn't get finished with dinner until nine. Of course, we'd gone to the Fish House, so we didn't even get there until nearly eight.''

"Please bear with me a moment, Esther, and tell me who drove.''

"Well, I went with Miriam and Mindy, and the men went in another car with Diane. I'd forgotten Diane, second alto. She lives over near Dave.''

"I see. Did you notice if Miriam made any phone calls at dinner?''

"I trust you're going to tell me why all this is important, Anna. No, she didn't, but she slipped into the rectory office and called before we left. To let Marvin know she was going out.''

"She said or you overheard?''

"Oh, she said. Miriam always includes everyone in her plans.''

"Have you seen the paper yet?''

"No, I always get mine at the airport newsstand. What's wrong?''

"William Brighton was beaten half to death last night.''

"Oh, Lord! His poor parents! Is he going to be all right?''

"Between you and me, I'll be surprised if he makes it.''

"You sound as if you've seen him.''

"I found him last night. Just a few minutes after nine.''

"How awful for you!''

"It made an impression, rather a lasting one, I'm afraid. I'm sorry now that I mentioned him at the rehearsal."

"Because of Miriam, you mean? Don't take Miriam too seriously."

"It's still awkward. Someone had been through all his photographs. Do you suppose she's the only one who might have been interested?"

There was a long pause. "No," said Esther Reed very positively. "I'm sure she wasn't the only one."

I didn't like the sound of that, but as Esther refused to add anything more, I said good-bye and dialed the Greenes'. A bright recorded message assured me that either Miriam or Marvin would be delighted to return my call, before a woman with a heavy Spanish accent picked up and told me that Mrs. Greene would be back in the afternoon.

I thanked her and tried next for Peter Laurimer, but the school secretary said he wouldn't arrive until 12:30. I remembered that Esther had said he gave private lessons, as well as teaching classes at the school, so I drove across town and along the river to a steep hill overlooking the Sound.

Peter Laurimer had a small, dark, Victorian-Gothic cottage. In back was a little barn, which I guessed was his studio. There were two cars in the drive, a dark Ford and a spiffy green Jaguar. I went down the road a way, parked, and waited until the Jag left a half hour later. Then I returned to the Laurimers'. I could hear a TV and children in the house, and as I neared the barn, the sound of a piano and the start of a scale. I knocked on the door; Peter, wearing a shirt and jeans, opened it.

"I'm Anna Peters. We've met a couple of times. Do you have a minute to talk?"

He looked at his watch. "I have another lesson at eleven. Then I have to go right to school."

"Half an hour's time enough."

"I'd hoped to do a little practicing. We're performing this Friday."

"I'm hoping to hear you," I said, stepping inside uninvited. "You've heard, of course, about the Brighton boy?"

"Brighton?" Peter Laurimer put on a puzzled look that I found unconvincing. "I'm afraid he's not one of my—"

"A suspect in the Urson killing. Tall, blond, a bit disconnected." I looked around as I spoke. Laurimer's studio was handsome and well appointed with a piano, an electric keyboard, music stands, tape recorders, and variously sized and shaped instrument cases. I was surprised, for from the description of his work life, I'd envisioned a hand-to-mouth existence.

"Doesn't ring a bell—I deal with so many kids," Peter said.

"This one was a protege, if that's the right word, of Bradley Urson's. A neighbor for a while of Angela Browning's."

"Maybe you could get to the point."

I had the feeling "Angela" was the key word. "If you remember, Brighton came up in the conversation at rehearsal the other day. He seems to be something of a freelance photographer."

"I don't see what this has to do with me," Peter said.

"Maybe nothing. The thing is, someone nearly killed the boy last night."

"In Branch Hill?"

"The outer reaches—he was the caretaker at the marina along the river."

"Robbery?"

"Undoubtedly. But not money. Photographs."

"You're putting me on."

"No. They were strewn all over the place. I think he was injured by someone who thought he knew more than he's told about the Urson case."

"Well, according to Angela, that's your business, isn't it? Investigations and that sort of thing." His voice trailed off as if he realized he'd made a mistake in bringing her up.

"Angela may know something as well."

Laurimer's face changed. He didn't wrinkle his brow or turn down his lips, but a kind of stillness came over him as if he were suddenly completely alert.

"I thought you might be able to help me on that," I said.

"In what way?"

"You know her well?"

"She's the best student I've ever had. Or am likely to have."

"That doesn't quite answer the question."

He flushed a little. "I've taught her for a year, a year and a half, actually."

"And she's fond of you. It's clear she looks up to you."

"As much as an adolescent can."

"She strikes me as rather an unusual adolescent. An unusually precocious one."

"A great talent sometimes has that effect," Laurimer said.

"I think she may be in danger."

"How could she be? In a town like this?"

"One child has been murdered. William Brighton was very nearly killed. When I visited him yesterday afternoon, I saw he was frightened. Like Angela."

"Angela can be melodramatic," Laurimer said, but I sensed that he was disturbed.

"What's your personal relationship with Angela?"

"What?"

"Your personal relationship with Angela?"

"I don't know what you're insinuating, but I'm ending this conversation right now."

"I saw you meet Angela in town the other day. I'd had the feeling she'd cut school to see you."

"Oh, that!" Laurimer was so relieved he gave a little laugh. "Yes, I did meet her. She said you'd treated her to lunch. Contributing to delinquency, Ms. Peters. It was quite accidental. Angela—" he considered his phrasing for a moment. "Angela needs a bit of guidance. Her parents are disengaged, if you know what I mean. Martha's raised Angela, but now she's at the stage where she needs a little fatherly advice. I drove her straight back to school, I assure you."

"It's not me you need to assure."

"Meaning?"

"Meaning it doesn't take psychic powers to sense the competitive jealousy around the Madrigal Society. Meaning that's not the best environment for an impressionable adolescent."

"Competition for the director's approval is the curse of amateur musicians."

"I'm not sure the average person would buy that explanation. What does one see? That Angela is gorgeous, that Mrs. Greene is jealous, that you—"

"Let's stop this right here. Angela is fourteen, and I don't like your insinuation."

"Angela is also terrified."

Laurimer's anger died out as suddenly as if I'd hit him. "It's true she hasn't been herself, but I guess the business with the Urson girl hit her harder than we'd thought."

"She blames herself in some way for Lindsay's death. I'd guess she isn't eating right. But it's more than grief. Something is troubling Angela, and I thought you might know what."

"I can't help you."

"You're sure?"

"I really must get to work. I don't know anything more."

"If I were you, I'd make it my business to find out," I said.

I walked back to my car, dissatisfied with myself. I had the feeling that I was losing my touch and I sat a few minutes reviewing my approach. I was about to write off the visit when the Ford shot out of the drive with no more than a hesitation at the highway. It looked as if Peter Laurimer had just canceled his eleven o'clock lesson.

I started my car and followed him into town, where he pulled into one of the municipal parking-lot entrances. I took the next one and saw him heading into the mall as I parked my car. When I got inside, Peter was at a phone booth, and I kept an eye on him through one of the display windows. He had a brief but animated conversation, hung up, and dialed again. This conversation was even briefer. He made two more phone calls, then checked his watch and hurried out to his car. From the mall entrance, I watched him turn in the direction of home. He'd apparently thought it worthwhile to come all the way to the center for a private phone call. I found that very interesting.

FOURTEEN

THE GREENES' HOUSE was large and lavish, decorated with both cash and flash. Miriam met me in a black-and-white striped hallway as big as a decent-sized apartment bedroom. There were well-framed mirrors and pictures on the walls, antique gilt tables, and a black marble floor to set off the lady of the house, who was dressed in a vivid green shift with chunky black jade beads. I was to be denied a glimpse of the famous hands, however; she was wearing a pair of rubber gloves, pink ones with red "nails" on the fingers.

"Oh, Anna! It is Anna, isn't it? What a nice surprise! I'm afraid I'm hardly fit for company," she said with a little smirk that told me she was sure every hair was in place.

"I was passing and thought I'd take a chance you were back."

"You just caught me. I dashed home from the Wetlands Board to do some repotting. I'm to do the flowers for the reception after the Madrigal Society concert."

"Don't let me hold you up."

"Come through to the kitchen," Miriam said.

She led the way to a baronial expanse done up with imported cabinetry, an industrial-size range, and a great many lights. The countertops were granite, as was the massive table that, at the moment, was covered with newspapers, peat, and potting soil. Half a dozen azaleas were arrayed on one side, along with two pretty cinereria.

"Good-looking plants," I said.

"I'd have a greenhouse if I had time," Miriam said, "but the Madrigal Society takes up so much time and so does entertaining." She had an odd habit of stressing all the syllables of important words.

"Were you trained as a singer?"

"Yes, as a matter of fact. I studied at the Conservatory, the New England Conservatory. But music's so uncertain. You need the real buccaneer spirit to make a career in the arts."

When she smiled, Miriam's perfect teeth gleamed with not a crack, not a chip, not the faintest stain. From head to toe she had a glossy, almost impossible perfection, which given her thirty-some or forty-some years, made one think of Dorian Gray and minor pacts with the dark powers.

"Of course, I had other opportunities." She held up her hands as she spoke. "I had a very good modeling career, and I've been so fortunate. The Madrigal Society and dear Peter have just been lifesavers. A real chance to grow." She stretched her arms as she spoke, throwing her head back like a satisfied lioness, and I understood a little better why Peter Laurimer might have proved elusive.

"Peter Laurimer seems very talented."

"Oh, indeed! Although he had to be pushed into the Society." She nodded for emphasis. "Like most men, he needs a push. I'd been talking the idea up for some time before he arrived. Of course, he's the maestro. It's only proper he gets the credit."

"He certainly has a feeling for period music."

"He lives in the seventeenth century. Positively lives there. A man it's been a privilege to know. In so many ways." Miriam gave one of the pots a sharp smack on the table, loosening its azalea.

"Someone else said that about him," I said. "Who was it? Maybe Angela. When I stayed with the Brownings last spring."

"Angela is an impressionable child," Miriam said coldly. "She can't expect to have an understanding of a man like Peter. A real artist."

"She does have a marvelous voice."

"Singing isn't just the voice," Miriam said with accents on every syllable in sight. "It's a way of life."

"You don't care for Angela?"

"Angela's so young, so full of herself."

Perhaps youth was Angela's real crime. "I've heard you were fond of another member of the Browning family."

"Ken? You have been listening to neighborhood gossip. Ken is a compulsive philanderer. Positively a Don Juan. The sort one encourages at one's peril."

"You sound as if you speak from experience."

"He claimed I broke his heart," she said impatiently. "Nonsense, of course, but I hate that sort of emotional blackmail."

"Was this last spring by any chance?"

"My dear, I was pursued summer, winter, and spring!" Miriam said, which was a nice way of leaving the dates vague. "But if I've learned one thing," she continued, "I've learned the power of selfishness. Oh, I suppose people thought I was selfish as a girl. I was pretty, elegant, a top model, but I still did an awful lot of things because other people expected them, wanted them from me. We women are trained to please, aren't we?" She gave an odd smile. "It took me years to see that pleasing is beside the point. You have to be yourself and that means doing what pleases you, not what pleases others."

"Even if it's not good?"

"We're talking about art, not morality," said Miriam, who was a philosophical femme fatale. "But I don't think it matters. We are what we are, and we have to live that way." She set the pot down and looked at me with her large, brilliant eyes.

"But one loses all hope of improvement."

She laughed then. "You're as naive as Peter. And you're a private investigator!"

"Is Peter naive?"

Miriam turned cautious. "You're very interested in Peter," she said.

"I'm interested in the Madrigal Society," I said. "And in Branch Hill. An odd town, don't you think?"

"Odd? Exclusive, certainly. And comfortable. Odd, I don't know."

"It's full of frightened children."

"I'm not fond of children," Miriam said. "Marvin has three from his first marriage, thank God. I told him he'd already burdened posterity sufficiently."

"William Brighton was frightened."

"William should have been frightened with the life he led."

"What do you mean?"

"Oh, I don't *know,* you understand. But I've got a damn good idea from what I've heard."

"And what did you hear?"

"You sound as if you're still on duty, Anna, but, of course, poor Scotty is in the clear now. With the *terrible* events of last night. I called Dottie this morning as soon as I read the paper. She was so relieved. I *know* they're completely satisfied. You can go home with a clear conscience to that wonderful painter of yours."

"Alex and Dottie are satisfied. I'm not sure I am."

"No point in being obsessive," Miriam said. "There's a point where we face the Mystery of Existence." I could hear the capital letters.

"My mystery isn't quite so global. I'm still interested in what happened to Lindsay Urson, a matter that has kind of gotten put to one side."

"She was a sweet little thing, no doubt," Miriam said, "but scarcely memorable. She was the kind of person who gets mislaid, forgotten."

"I doubt her parents have forgotten."

"I suppose now the police will be after Bradley."

"About William?"

"Who else? For two reasons."

"Two?"

"Dear, he's gay or I'm a Martian. Lover's quarrel. They never last long with Bradley. He's so serious. Young men like that aren't serious. They'd rather put out, get paid, and be done with it. In my professional life I saw a lot like William and Bradley."

"Maybe yours were less idealistic than Bradley?"

"Less hypocritical. I've got no patience with Bradley Urson."

I shook my head. "I don't see it that way."

"No?" Her voice was sharp.

"I think it had something to do with the photos."

"What photos?"

"You brought them up yourself—at rehearsal, remember? William's camera, his inconvenient candid shots."

"There was nothing personal about that, but I'd heard. Some of the rumors about that boy are hardly repeatable."

"I understand you went to see Lindsay Urson at her gymnastics club just before she died."

"Who told you that? Why would I have gone to a smelly gym to see a child who lived virtually next door?"

"As I heard it, you believed she had some photos. Photos from William Brighton."

Miriam laughed. It was a throaty laugh with just enough rasp to be unpleasant. "Incriminating photos?"

"It crossed my mind."

"You should stay in Branch Hill, Anna! The place needs livening up! He took some snaps of our dog, Snooker. And of our Persian cat."

I envisioned a black, self-satisfied cat with eyes like Miriam's.

"You don't believe me?"

"In my business you have to suspend belief—or disbelief."

"A very scientific profession," Miriam said and laughed again.

"William wasn't beaten half to death for animal photos," I said.

"I've told you, Bradley Urson—"

"I found William. Whoever hurt him was after his photos—they were strewn all over the place."

"You'd gone back to see him again?" Miriam asked. I might have been mistaken, but I thought she was unpleasantly surprised.

Now it was my turn to smile. "I wanted to ask him about his camera," I said, "and about his 'portrait of Branch Hill.'"

I MARKED DOWN Miriam's interview as a draw. I didn't know much more about her relations with Angela, Bradley, Ken, or William than I had before, but I felt I knew a bit more about her. I decided that her society dreadnaught manner was just a pose and that she was both more intelligent and more forceful than I'd guessed. I wondered if she'd be able to produce some pet photos if need be and whether or not she was one of the people Laurimer had called.

Of course, unless Esther had lied about the dinner party, Miriam was in the clear as far as William was concerned, but I couldn't help wondering if she had really called her husband and what that conversation had been about. And it wasn't beyond possibility that it was Marvin who'd wanted some photos back, especially as he and Miriam were each other's alibis for the night of the Urson murder. The "special atmosphere" of Branch Hill was beginning to get to me, and I thought a visit to the Brownings might be in order. But though it was getting close to five, no one was home. I decided to meet the commuter train and see if I could have a word with Ken.

I recognized his BMW convertible in the station parking lot and went inside to phone the hospital to check on William. Then I bought a copy of the local weekly, *Hillside,* and sat down to wait. I read a pre-

view of the Madrigal Society's season opening concert, which promised "more of the superb period
music the Society is renowned for" and news of
Bradley Urson's Boys Club outing to the city.

The *Hillside* favored lots of adjectives and a certain
coziness of style that had begun to irritate me long
before the six-twenty was announced and its single
headlight appeared far down the graceful curve that
skirted the cove. There weren't any passengers waiting to get on, and I had no trouble picking Ken out of
the business-suited crowd disembarking with their
briefcases and evening papers. He clambered down the
steps awkwardly, his right hand supported by a sling.

"Hello, Ken."

"Oh, Anna," he said in a distracted way. "I hadn't
realized you were in town."

"Just for a few days. I'm still working on the case."

"I'm beginning to think of moving farther up-
state," Ken said, "the way things are going. That
Brighton kid last night. It was clear he was trouble
from the start."

"He had very serious injuries."

"Sure. Get guys like that living in town—who
knows what follows. Someone came after him. God
knows what else they got up to."

Ken set down his case and tried to shrug his jacket
over his shoulders. I reached out to help him. His right
hand was completely concealed in a thick white cast,
but I noticed that his left was also bruised and swollen.

"Thanks," Ken said. "Damn nuisance. I'd better
call Isabel. I'm not sure I'm going to be able to drive.
I have a manual shift."

"Is it broken?"

"Hairline fracture. Hurts like hell. The codeine they gave me has worn off."

"I can drive you home," I said.

"Oh, thanks. But aren't you waiting for a train? My mental processes aren't working too well. I wouldn't have gone in to work at all if I hadn't had to make a presentation."

"I was hoping to see you, actually."

"Well! I am flattered," Ken said with a trace of his usual flirtatiousness. His face was flushed, and I decided he'd had a few drinks on the train. He looked around. "I half expected Branch Hill's finest."

"Why was that?"

"Just routine. Some kid gets beaten up and all our lives are disrupted." He picked up his case and we started for the stairs.

"How did you hurt your hand?"

"Shut it in the car hood this morning. Don't say it, stupidest thing I could have done. The car was acting funny, a bit sluggish, and when I got to the station, I opened the hood to take a look. I guess I just didn't get the prop set right. I was listening to the engine with both hands resting right where the hood comes down and whamo! By the time I reached the city, my right hand was swollen up like a melon."

"You're lucky you didn't break both."

"That's what the doctor said. This one's sore, too, but I guess, automatic, you know, you lift the right hand first—it took the worst of it."

Ken was right-handed; I guessed that if he had attacked William, his right hand would have showed the most damage. Possibly a break? Had he deliberately closed his hand in the car to mask other damage? Or was I becoming as paranoid as the residents of Branch Hill?

"Let me get the door for you. Shall I put your case in the back?"

"No, there's room here. Just barely." He struggled one-handed with his seat belt until I reached over and snapped it closed. "I never rent these damn compacts," Ken said.

"My clients appreciate them."

He laughed. "Old Alex would, anyway. Old Alex. Good old New England thrift."

"Alex is about to become an ex-client. He feels that the attack on William just about clears Scott."

"Yeah, that's how it'll play here. It's blaming the victim, of course, but William's the outsider. Even though he's a rich boy, a Greenwich kid—for all that he's still the outsider and better him than a Branch Hill suspect. And there wasn't much to choose between them, was there? I mean evidence-wise."

"That's all fine if William was the one who killed Lindsay."

"Rough justice?"

"Yes. But if he wasn't—"

"Oh, I don't think Branch Hill will worry too much about the subtleties."

"I was thinking of something more practical."

Ken looked over at me, instantly alert. "Like?"

"That leaves the murderer still at large. And still dangerous."

"The police have about ruled out any kind of serial killer."

"Me too. But I'm worried about something else. I'm convinced that the Urson killing was a mistake."

"A mistake? What do you mean, a mistake?"

"I mean Lindsay was not the target. She was mistaken for someone else."

Ken went pale. "That's a damn wild idea."

"Is it? No one has ever come up with a motive for Lindsay's death. Sex wasn't a motivation. Nor drugs. She had no boyfriend, no enemies. If it had been pure impulse, the spur of the moment, I think there would have been subsequent killings."

Ken groped in his pocket, found a pack of cigarettes, and fumbled one from the pack to his lips without lighting it.

"You haven't asked me who the target was," I said. "Does that mean you know?"

Ken took the cigarette out of his mouth and began twisting it between his fingers. "Dear God," he said after a minute. "What are we going to do?"

"I'd arrange protection for Angela, if I were you. Plus, I'd speak to the police. And I'd get her to a good doctor."

He looked at me. "What do you mean about a doctor?"

"How much weight has she lost since I was here last? Ten pounds, fifteen, twenty? She's skin and bones, not that she was fat to begin with. And the business the other night—that temporary disappearance. Did you ever find out what that was about?"

"I was out," said Ken. "I had dinner in the city with a friend and didn't get back until late."

"Better start staying home."

He recovered himself at that suggestion. "I think you're wildly over-reacting. I'm not about to sign on as a client, if that's what you're hinting. Kids—you don't have kids, you don't know—but who the hell knows what they get up to? Stages. They go through the damnedest stages."

"I neither need nor want your business," I said. "I just don't like to see little girls frightened."

"Hell, that's why I moved to the Estates in the first place. I was just trying to protect my family. And now—"

"And now there's someone dangerous around town." We'd passed the start of the thick stone wall around the Estates, and I slowed down and pulled over to the curb within sight of the control booth. "It's funny, but I've thought you might know who."

"Me?"

"Yes. All that story about slipping out late at night to meet a friend. I think that was all nonsense. You were out earlier, probably."

"How the hell would I have done that with eight for dinner?"

"You were in and out of the kitchen. So helpful with the dinner arrangements, getting ice, getting wine, checking on the next course. It even took your wife by surprise."

"I was making an effort to be hospitable, to give Isabel a hand. Jesus! Everything gets twisted around."

"My thought was you went out the back door to speak to someone. Maybe to set up that little rendez-vous, which, I think, had been on but was canceled."

"So why the hell would I have mentioned going out to you in the first place?"

I put the car back in gear and headed for the gate house. "You were drunk," I said. "And you'd been acting so nervous and guilty about the police that you felt you'd better give me a reason. That's why."

"So what do you think happened? I went out and killed Lindsay?"

"No. But I think you may have seen the person who did. And I think William saw him as well."

"Is that what you think?"

"Yes. And it was a damn smart thing you injured your right hand."

"Why's that?"

"Because William Brighton died this afternoon at two-thirty."

FIFTEEN

By Friday, the day of the Madrigal Society concert, I was out of favor with Branch Hill in general, and with Detective Lieutenant Canelli and Alex Valon in particular. It seemed that members of the Branch Hill community (the Lieutenant's phrase) had been calling to complain of my activities. I felt they might better have complained about two murders in six months, but this view did nothing to soften Canelli. He was as allergic to ruffled feathers as Alex, who'd wailed earlier in the morning, "The Greenes are our neighbors."

"Right. And for that reason, one or both of them must be considered suspects. Along with all the other nice folks who are of age."

"Really, in light of recent developments—"

"Alex, if it wasn't Scott, it must have been someone else. William, in light of recent developments, as you put it, probably wasn't the one. I think—"

"Anna, are you working for the Brownings?"

"You know me better than that. I'm employed by you and only by you until the case is closed."

"It's closed now as far as I'm concerned," Alex said. "And I'm going to have a word with Tosh Stoughton and tell him so, too."

I'm sure he'd done just that, because when I belatedly went in to make my statement to Canelli, he got onto the same subject. "Folks have been bending the

Chief's ear virtually since you got into town," the detective said. "It doesn't make for civic tranquility."

"As they say, no pain, no gain. I've come up with something interesting."

Canelli managed to restrain his enthusiasm.

"I should have given you this the other night, but in all the excitement I forgot I'd picked it up." I passed him the photo.

When he didn't react, I said, "That's a photo of Lindsay Urson and Angela Browning. It was on the floor. The fingerprints are mine. I'd gone to wash my hands, saw it, and picked it up."

"That was evidence," he said. "What the hell did you remove it for?"

"It gave me a shock. Then I heard the sirens and must have stuck it in my pocket. I only found it when I got back to my room. I've shown it to Bradley Urson."

"So?"

"I think it bothered him. He'd rather there was a reason for his daughter's death—I mean beyond a coincidence that she looked like another girl."

"You can't build a case on coincidence," Canelli said.

"You don't have a motive, though, do you? You've just lost a suspect. I doubt you have any other leads."

"We're developing a case," he said grimly. "That takes time. And it's an awful lot easier without interference."

He delivered various other warnings while I checked and signed my statement.

"I imagine you'll be heading back south today," he said as I got up to leave. "Mr. Valon tells us that your

employment with him has definitely been termi-
nated.''

"You imagine wrong. I'm going to the Madrigal
Society concert tonight. A really high-quality ensemble. Have you heard them?''

"I'm not much on classical music.''

"You should make their acquaintance.''

"And you should go home, Ms. Peters.''

With this atmosphere, I knew there was no point in
asking what they'd uncovered about Marvin Greene
or whether they'd managed any interest in Ken
Browning's amorous adventures. I decided, instead,
that it was time to talk to the vigilant Davis, gateman
at the Estates. Davis had taken a certain amount of
heat last spring, and I thought he might be less discreet about the Estates habitués than he had been pre-
viously.

I wasn't in a very good mood myself. Canelli had
some legitimate, as well as illegitimate, reasons for
being upset with me. He was quite right that these
cases need careful and detailed work, but of neces-
sity, I'd had to blunder along and try to stir something up. I liked to think that the attack on William
would have come anyway, but if my ideas were right
about the case, I'd unintentionally precipitated that—
and possibly put Angela and others in danger as well.
There was something else, too: I hadn't done this sort
of work for a while. Executive Security had evolved
into a company that makes arrangements, takes pre-
cautions, keeps trouble from happening. As a result,
I'd gotten comfortable with maps and schedules, balance sheets, printouts, and information gathering, and
I was beginning to think that maybe this visit had been

foolish. I should have told Alex I was sorry, insisted he contact a local detective, and preserved both dignity and friendship.

I was maundering along in this way when I happened to glance in my rearview mirror, which was filled by a green and white Branch Hill police cruiser. As I was crawling through traffic in the center of town, I didn't think any more about it, but when I took the highway en route to the Estates, the cruiser turned, too, and again when I reached the road to the development. As I pulled up beside the gate house, he slowed, and I guessed correctly that he would turn around and park in the vicinity. At first I was irritated, feeling I had enough trouble without such childish harassment, and then I had another thought that cheered me quite a bit: Canelli and company were hedging their bets and waiting to see if some other sludge might come to the surface.

Davis opened the door of his kiosk as I approached. "Can I help you?" he asked. Then he frowned, as if puzzled.

"Anna Peters," I said, taking out one of my cards. "My husband and I stayed for nearly a week with the Brownings last spring."

"Oh, yes," he said. "Good to see you again. I recognized your face, but I couldn't think of your name. Visiting someone today?"

"No, I wanted to speak to you for a moment."

He held open the door and stepped aside.

"Thanks. This is cozy." The kiosk was larger than it looked. There was room for a counter on two sides, a substantial desk chair, half a dozen small monitors, a computer with printer, a phone, a coffee machine, a pile of newspapers and magazines, a large map of the estates, a heater, and a board with small lights representing each of the Estates houses.

"All the comforts of home," he said, folding down an extra chair for me. I noticed he used only his left hand. "Care for some coffee?"

"Yes, please. I wasn't sure Total Protection would still be here. There was some question last spring, wasn't there?"

"That's an understatement. I'm still not sure we won't lose the contract renewal unless there's a break in the case."

"How long have you worked for them?"

"Ten years. Five of them right here. I was on the force in Bridgeport, but I had to retire early. Partial disability."

"Your arm?"

"Shoulder. All those Westerns where people get shot in the shoulder and barely miss a step are way outta line."

"I can imagine. I don't know if you're aware that I was hired by the Valons to see what I could find out about the Urson case."

"Mr. Valon's been very concerned about Scott."

"Yes. Though less so now. He's convinced that the attack on William Brighton pretty much clears the boy."

"But you aren't so sure?"

"I never seriously thought Scott was involved. But there's no proof one way or the other, and I'm still interested in what did happen. I wonder if you'd remember who came in and out that night?"

"Not that I'd be likely to forget," Davis said, "but in any case, it's all on the disks."

He tapped the computer. "We put a hard disk in just a year ago. Now everything's stored right here."

"And you actually log each car that comes in and out?"

"Sure thing. I'll show you." He sat down at the computer and typed in the date of Lindsay's murder. In seconds, a column of license plate numbers and times filled the screen. "What time are you interested in?"

"Eleven thirty to two A.M."

Davis scrolled down. He used military time: 22:20, 22:49, 23:11, 23:59. "There you are. BMW 456 CJV. Out at a minute to midnight."

"When did he come back in?"

"Let's see." The cursor moved down the line. "Twelve-twenty. I remember now, he stopped on the way in. Said he'd been out getting cigarettes."

Davis sniffed as he said this and raised his eyebrows.

I wondered why Ken had told me he'd been out until nearly two A.M., and asked if he often went out at night on small errands.

"Couple times a week at least, but he was rarely back so quick."

"I think I see the picture. Any other cars show the same pattern?"

Davis didn't answer, but thought a moment then called up the data for two days before. I watched the numbers appear. The BMW went out at midnight on the dot, an LC 2356M went out at 00:05. Both cars returned two hours later within ten minutes of each other.

"What's an LC?"

"Lincoln Continental." He punched up several other dates with the same pattern, a regular Tuesday and Thursday schedule.

"Miriam Greene?" I asked.

"You didn't hear it from me," Davis warned.

I nodded. "And this was all available. The police have seen all of this?"

"Sure. They took copies of everything."

"The murder was a Tuesday. Supposedly she should have met Ken that night."

Davis shrugged.

"And since then?"

"Not so's I've noticed. Let's take a look." He had a Find function that enabled him to pick out license number and time combinations. "I've a lot of time to play with the machine," he said. "No, see, here's two nights after. He's out, she's out—but she's back within forty-five minutes. That's it."

"They broke it off."

"Look like it. 'Course with Mrs. Greene, nobody lasts too long. That's a restless lady."

"Does Peter Laurimer ever come around? An older brown Ford, plate number BT4605?"

"That's the music teacher, right?"

"Right, and unless I'm mistaken, another good friend of Mrs. Greene's."

"I don't find him."

"Was she or her husband out at all the night of the murder?"

"That I can tell you from memory. They were both home."

"Just one last thing. What about last Wednesday night?"

Davis tapped in the date. "What time are we talking?"

"What time did Ken Browning usually get home from work?"

"He catches the 6:20. Unless the train's late, he's home by 6:45 or so."

"Let's start there."

The numbers scrolled steadily toward the top of the screen. "Wait. That's the Continental, right? What time is that?"

"21:35."

"They went out to dinner at the Fish House after madrigal practice."

"Here's Ken. 21:20. That's 9:20 P.M."

"Was that unusual?"

Davis shrugged. "He sometimes stayed late in the city. More usually a Friday. The Mrs. would meet him in New York for a show or something."

"And he didn't come back and go out. You're sure of that?"

"Look for yourself," Davis said.

"The business with Miriam Greene—that wasn't exactly a secret, was it?"

"Not to anyone with eyes."

"That's what I thought." I thanked Davis, shook his hand, and returned to my car. I had more questions than I'd come with, and I hoped the Madrigal Society concert would provide some answers.

THE CONCERT WAS HELD ten miles away in another waterside town with a beautiful eighteenth-century church. I'd called and asked Esther Reed if she wanted a ride, but she already had a standing offer from one of the second violins. I spent some time on the phone with Harry, annoying him about his diet, then set off to find the place. As it turned out, I arrived a half hour early, in plenty of time to admire the severely elegant church.

It had a pale gray and white interior, fine ornamental woodwork, a large, well-wrought brass chandelier, and a pre-modern air of serenity and self-confidence. There was nothing out of place and nothing extraneous, an admirable aesthetic—although the modern bottom would have appreciated a seat cushion. After I had examined the interior for a few minutes, I decided to take a little walk. I left just as the members of the small accompanying string ensemble began wandering in and out, checking that their music was in place and gossiping in the doorways.

Outside the mild weather still held, and only a few of the ash trees were considering fall. The church was directly on the green, and it did look pretty, rising over the trees in neat white geometry to a Bulfinch-style spire. The audience was arriving and, as the parking lot and the street filled up, a few bolder souls were parking their cars on the grass.

I checked my watch, saw there were still fifteen minutes left, and walked through the parking lot. The lights were on all over the church and the attached hall and, with floodlights mounted rather haphazardly around the property, there was plenty of light. At the back, a late, old-fashioned rosebush was blooming in what I supposed had been the yard of the parish house. I was admiring the light, sweet scent of the pale blossoms when a door opened and closed at the back of the church.

"...do something. You've promised and promised! We can't wait—"

"I've told you, everything's nearly ready."

"...nearly ready for two weeks! And look what's happened. I'm so scared!" I was sure that was Angela.

"It's all right. Nothing will happen to you. Not when I'm here. You understand that, don't you?"

"Yes—it's just—with William—" Her voice dropped and the man's did, too.

"...not necessarily...know that."

"He's been...acting funny."

"Has she said anything? Anything at all? I think you're..."

"...knows. I'm sure Anna knows."

"What difference does it make to us?"

"I just want to get away. Don't you? How can you stand this?"

He whispered something unintelligible, then said, "I've got to go in. They'll all notice if I'm not in there," and I knew it was Peter Laurimer.

SIXTEEN

THE CONCERT WAS beautiful and disturbing, with glorious voices and melancholy lyrics. "O hear my crying," the poet pleaded. "O I faint. O I die...." The voices of the chorus blended as smoothly as brandy in cream, and Angela's soprano, untouched by that Jacobean double entendre, rose pure and serious. Her extraordinary talent rested not only on her instrument but on her unusual concentration and conviction. The nervous, rather flippant teenager disappeared completely when she sang, and another personality, harder, brighter, more insistent, emerged. Esther had said that Laurimer lived in the seventeenth century, but Angela, too, lived far away and when they sang Dowland's "Come again, sweet love doth now invite," they seemed transported to their real home.

Clearly Laurimer was being foolish, if not criminal, but I could see that he had his reasons. He was serious, a bit unworldly, boyish, and dreamy, and despite her age, Angela easily would have been cast as his *belle dame*. As for Angela, I guessed she had been only too eager, for there was an emptiness about her life that she was too intelligent not to have sensed. Laurimer, the Madrigal Society, Art with a capital 'A' would have added some emotional sustenance to the chilly opulence of Branch Hill.

Still, she and Peter had not chosen the happiest of artistic residences. The seventeenth century had seen the downside of love, and, on reflection, many of the madrigal lyrics made me uneasy: "To see, to hear, to touch, to kiss, to die" did not seem wholesome, and, in the present atmosphere, the nexus of love, death, and danger struck me as ominous.

I WENT TO the reception in a somber mood and had to exert myself to appear festive. Around me was a chorus of "Marvelous, simply marvelous" and "Beautiful, just beautiful."

"I'd like to talk to you," I said to Angela.

"Not now. I can't concentrate on anything now. After a performance my mind's just empty."

I wondered if those airs would eventually hamper her work. "It's important."

"I'll call you." She waved over my shoulder. "There's Martha! Weren't we marvelous?"

She slipped away with only a glance at Laurimer, who was looking exhausted and happy, his face damp with perspiration. I had a word with Esther and left early. Outside the overheated church, the stars glittered beyond the halo of arc lights and city shine. My car was cold, and, though I let it warm up for a moment, it continued to sputter and cough sporadically every time I had to stop. I thought it would be all right once I left town, and, sure enough, the engine settled down long enough to get me out along a deserted stretch of salt marsh and meadow. Then it suddenly lost compression, and I found myself slowing irresistibly to a stop. I still had half a tank of gas, but the oil light was glowing and a variety of little round warning lights were blinking on the computerized dashboard.

Damn! The nearest light showed a wet reflection in the marshland to my left, while to the right, the river side was a dark, unbroken expanse of salt meadow. Although I couldn't have been more than a couple of miles from the center of Branch Hill, I had apparently chanced upon one of the last pockets of open land on that overdeveloped coast, and I was wearing dress pumps unsuitable for a ramble.

I put on my flashers and popped the hood, deciding to test my slender mechanical knowledge. The engine seemed hot, and when I cautiously started to open the radiator, I heard a warning rumble of steam. Great! There was water all around but I had no container, and there didn't look to be any neighbors in sight. I was debating whether to wait for help and for the radiator to cool or to start hiking in the general direction of Branch Hill, when a car slowed behind me. I turned toward the dazzling lights and felt a moment's apprehension as a big black Continental stopped. A tinted window slid down with an electronic buzz. Ken Browning leaned out and asked, "Need some help?"

Miriam Greene was at the wheel. "We thought it was you. What happened?"

"I don't know," I said. "The car was cold and cranky all through town, then it seemed to be all right, then it died. I'll have to find a phone and call the company."

"Get in," said Ken. "We can give you a lift." He spoke unusually slowly, every word steeped in alcohol. "Miriam was kind enough to give me a ride home. Angela and Isabel will be there all night."

I got into the back, and Miriam put the car in gear. "I didn't expect anywhere around here to be so deserted," I said.

"And of course no one would stop," Miriam said. "I almost didn't, but Ken never forgets a woman. He knew who you were right away."

"I was just deciding whether to wait or to walk."

"Not a good idea to walk," Ken said. "Not a good idea at all at night."

"No, I suppose not."

"Particularly here," Miriam said. "This road becomes River Street. Where the marina is." She glanced at Ken as she spoke. "You couldn't pay me to walk along there at night."

"The trouble with Miriam," Ken said, "is that she has no imagination. It always surprises her when there are messes."

"It surprises me how many you make," she said tartly.

Ken laughed. "Miriam doesn't understand people. Do you think that's true of all beautiful women?" He'd turned halfway round in his seat, and I could see the dead whiteness of his cast.

"Why should it be?" I asked.

"*Brava,*" said Miriam. "Ken pretends he doesn't know any other kind," she added over her shoulder to me.

"They never have to exert themselves," Ken said. "They live for their looks. To preserve their looks. It's so all-consuming they haven't room for anything else."

"What about handsome men?"

"Men are different," Ken said. His voice was sad.

Miriam laughed. "You can see he's hopeless."

"I am now," Ken said and fell into a morose silence.

A few lights appeared along the road, and I guessed we were on the outskirts of Branch Hill.

"You can drop me at the first public phone," I said.

"Nonsense," Miriam said. "You don't want to wait in the cold at some phone booth. They'll be hours. Ken and I are going to The Lobsterman for a drink. A drink for Ken and food for me. You can call from there."

"All right," I said, although I couldn't think of anything less pleasant than watching them rake over the ashes of their romance.

"We usually go to the Wharf Cafe opposite the marina, but Ken—"

"It's a filthy dive," Ken said abruptly. "Shut up about the marina."

"Such temperament," she said. "You should have been a singer, Ken. Didn't you think we were good tonight, Anna?"

"Outstanding."

"Odd, isn't it, how well such old music suits new situations? I sometimes wonder about that."

"No progress in emotions?" I suggested.

"'Ah, cruel love,'" she sang in her low, resonant voice, "'uncertain and brief are thy joys / And it even pleases thee / that the greatest happiness should end in tears.'"

"Jesus!" said Ken. "Haven't we heard enough for one evening?"

"Isn't that like a man? To complain you've lost interest in him when he lacks your interests."

"Miriam's interests come and go, regardless," Ken said, but the prospect of a drink seemed to have restored his equanimity. When we had reached The Lobsterman, he hustled into the bar, Miriam went to the ladies room, and I found the phone booth and dialed the car rental. They were apologetic but said that nothing could be done until the next day. I gave them the car's location as best I could and said I'd come by in the morning to see about a replacement.

"Any luck?" Miriam asked as I stepped out. In the dim lobby light, she looked more striking than ever. She had on the black silk with the silver beading she'd worn for the concert, very high heels, black stockings, long black kid gloves, and a beautiful black and silver Art Deco hair ornament like the Queen of the Night. It was just her luck that it wasn't a seventeenth-century look; she was one hundred percent modern and too old to be reshaped for an eccentric like Peter Laurimer.

"They'll take care of it tomorrow. I'm going to see about a cab."

"Come have a drink first. *Please*," Miriam said, turning confidential. "I wouldn't have given Ken a ride if I'd realized the state he's in."

I looked at my watch. "I'll order a cab for eleven," I said, but as it turned out, I was told I'd have to wait at least forty-five minutes and probably an hour.

With this cheerful news, I went into the restaurant part of The Lobsterman and joined Ken and Miriam at a corner table. Her long, black gloves lay like a pair of eels on the cloth between them, and she was tucking into a seafood salad. Ken had started a bottle of wine.

"I'm starving," Miriam said. "Don't mind me. Singing always makes me hungry."

"It's disgusting," Ken said. "She thinks of nothing but food since she started to diet."

"You wouldn't like me fat," Miriam said.

"It wasn't me who was complaining."

"As far as I know, no one was complaining," she said. The palpable tension between them didn't seem to bother her at all, and it crossed my mind that emotional heat—of whatever source—was what she needed.

"Don't give me that. I know why the diet, the new hair, the new clothes. All this black and purple—"

"If you know," Miriam said coldly, "there's no need to discuss it."

"There damn well is!"

"You're making Anna nervous. She's not interested in our quarrels."

Ken looked at me, as if he'd forgotten who I was or how I'd gotten there. "Don't be too sure," he said. "Anna's not satisfied." He smiled suddenly as if he'd had an idea. "Anna's curious and persistent."

"If I were you, I'd find that idea alarming," Miriam said.

"Why's that?" I asked.

"Ken lives an irregular life," Miriam said.

"Look who's talking. You know, I was happy until I met her." Ken poured himself another drink and looked at the diminished bottle sourly. "They've made these smaller with that damn metric system. You know that? I was pursued in my own backyard." He laughed too loudly.

"I didn't think the Estates had backyards," I said.

"'An uninterrupted parklike setting,'" Ken said. "And Miriam knows every inch of it, don't you, darling? That little clump of rhododendrons, the bridge by the old pond. The woods. Jesus, I thought she'd kill me off."

"There's no reason to be crude," Miriam said though she didn't seem at all embarrassed by these *al fresco* revelations.

"Anything goes with Miriam so long as her precious hands are protected. Look at them, they're so perfect, they're unnatural. It's the gloves that do it. Always those goddamn gloves. I must have been crazy. I have been crazy."

"What you've been is drunk," Miriam said in a dangerous voice. "When you're drinking, you lose perspective. You say stupid things and put yourself in stupid positions."

"For you!" he said. "It was for you!"

"Was it?"

"I ought to leave you," I said. "I'm sure my cab will be along soon."

"Your cab will be an hour—if you're lucky," Miriam said. "I thought you were interested in Branch Hill. Or do you just want the tourist's version? 'An executive community with the very best in amenities, a gracious lifestyle, excellent schools. A community for America's finest families.' Do you believe that? Ken does, don't you, Ken? This place is a pushover for realists, let me tell you, because everybody else has his head up his ass."

She pushed away her empty plate as she spoke and poured a little of Ken's wine into her glass. "He'll complain to me about this later," she said. "He'll say I treat him badly. But he won't stop bothering me. That's what I call being unrealistic."

"And are you realistic?" I asked when it became clear that Ken had lost either speech or interest.

"Very," she said.

Ken laughed. "Not if you have hopes of Peter Laurimer. That's who she prefers—Laurimer, an artsy-fartsy asshole if there ever was one."

"I didn't think we were discussing Peter," Miriam said with dignity.

"But Peter's numero uno," Ken said. "Peter's the key to everything."

"Including Lindsay Urson's murder?" I asked.

Miriam laughed, a very low, disagreeable sound. "Anna's truly obsessive. Poor Peter didn't even know the girl."

"He knows her friend Angela well enough."

"Don't start on Angela," Ken said, loudly enough so that people at the nearby tables turned their heads. "I don't want to talk about Angela with you—or Miriam."

"You don't want to face facts," I said.

"I've faced enough facts. Like that Miss Lovely Hands here has jerked me around long enough."

"You're such a child," Miriam said. The hotter he got, the calmer she became.

They traded insults for a bit until I got bored and said, "That's all as may be. My concern is Angela. You know my theory," I told Ken.

"Shut up about your theory," Ken said.

"A theory!" Miriam said with more than her usual emphasis. "Do tell!"

"I said, shut up!"

"Ken should have been born in Saudi Arabia," Miriam said.

"That Lindsay Urson was killed by mistake," I said.

"Rather a serious mistake," she said calmly, but her eyes had gone strange, very dark and glassy.

"Rather. And you see, I think that—"

But I didn't finish, because Ken stood up suddenly, jostling the table. The wine bottle fell over, splashing Miriam's dress, so that she jumped up, crying, "Oh, shit!" and scrambled for a napkin. Ken made a grab for me across the table, but I got myself out of the way, and put my heavy chair between us.

"Don't you mention my daughter! Don't you ever mention her!" he said, and other things that would have been more impressive had he been sober.

As the hostess came over, I saw her motioning to the big, solid-looking barman. "I'm afraid Mr. Browning isn't feeling well," I said. "And perhaps some clean water for Mrs. Greene's dress?"

Ken continued to denounce me and Miriam simultaneously, until Miriam slapped his face. There was a sudden embarrassed silence in which Ken sat down heavily and started to cry, and I made my way outside to look for my cab. It arrived a few minutes later, and, as we were pulling away, I saw Miriam and Ken walking arm in arm to her big Continental.

I GOT UP LATE the next morning, and by the time I had conducted my negotiations with the rental company, I'd missed the Seafarer's Inn's breakfast hours. To avoid troubling Mrs. Weaver, I took my complimentary morning papers and walked down to the diner for breakfast and then into town to pick up a new compact car. I had just gotten back when Esther Reed phoned.

"I'm so glad I caught you," she said.

"I had breakfast out."

"I need to talk to you. Can you come into the center?"

"Sure—unless we can talk on the phone."

"No, I'd rather tell you in person, if it's not too much trouble. I'm at the bank. The County Savings on Main. There's a lot in the back."

"All right, I'll be there in fifteen minutes."

"I really appreciate that, Anna. I'll see you then."

Puzzled, I hung up the phone, fetched my car, and made my way through the Saturday morning shopping traffic to the bank. Esther was standing outside the rear entrance, waiting for me, and as soon as she saw the car, she crossed the lot without waiting for me to park.

"Where to?" I asked as I opened the door.

"I'm not sure."

I found a space and shut off the engine.

"I probably shouldn't have bothered you," Esther said.

"I could do with a small problem, if that's what you're worried about."

She gave a little laugh. "I'm just hoping that's what this is." Then she took a deep breath and said, "I'm treasurer for the Madrigal Society and I handle all the money from ticket sales. If other members sell tickets in advance, they turn the proceeds over to me. That's routine, and I had quite a bit of cash last night, between the last of the advance sale money that was handed in and the receipts from the door. I hate to keep money around the house—in fact, I'd have been here at nine if I hadn't been tied up with a call from the airport. Anyway, when I got my receipt back, I found out that someone had cleaned out our account."

"Entirely?"

"Just about. I put in 2,950 dollars this morning. Our total now is 3,000 dollars and forty-eight cents. That's just over 700 dollars short, because we had 750-something last week."

"What happens to this money normally?"

"It goes to operating expenses, to reimburse Peter, as director, and to buy music. Anything left at the end of the year is divided—it usually amounts to a couple hundred dollars or so each."

"Who else has access to the account?"

"Just Peter and I. Miriam sometimes deposits—so does Peter. But Peter and I are the only ones who can make withdrawals."

"Did you ask the teller about withdrawals?"

"She said the record showed one this morning. That must have been right after the bank opened, because I was here by 10:15."

"Then I think we'd better go and see Peter Laurimer," I said.

Esther looked acutely uncomfortable. "Maybe there was a good reason. I'm sure there was—some unexpected emergency."

"All the more reason to get the matter cleared up. If there is a good reason, it would look odd if you hadn't caught it."

"I know that," she said. "We'd better go. I'm sure there's some explanation."

"Yes," I said, but I was thinking about Peter Laurimer's conversation with Angela and wondering what the two of them had cooked up.

SEVENTEEN

THE LAURIMERS' DRIVE was empty when we arrived. Esther said that Jill Laurimer would be out doing the shopping and led the way to Peter's studio. The door was locked, however, and when Esther knocked at the house, it was Jill, not Peter, who answered.

"How nice to see you, Esther," she said. "I thought it went very well last night."

Jill Laurimer was short and rather stocky, with a blunt, no-nonsense face under short blond hair. A girl of three or four had twined herself around one of her mother's legs, and from the kitchen came the excited sounds of other Laurimer offspring.

"Yes, it did. I think Peter was pleased," Esther said. "This is Anna Peters, Alex Valon's friend. She gave me a ride over. Is Peter home?"

Jill shook her head. "You haven't heard. Angela called and canceled her lesson—it was six-thirty or seven—she knows we're up early. Her dad was in an accident last night. Quite a bad one. They're all over at the hospital."

"He couldn't have been driving," Esther said. "He broke his hand."

"Miriam Greene was driving. They piled that big Continental into a phone pole on Hill Street. I imagine it was that bad curve where the school bus tipped over a few years ago."

"What about Miriam?" I asked.

"'Shook up' was what Angela said. It was the passenger's side that took the worst of it. And it's a big car."

"Oh, how terrible for the Brownings!" Esther said. "They've had enough trouble."

"If he hadn't been riding around with Miriam—"

"It was his hand," Esther said. "He wanted to get home early, and you know Isabel."

Jill Laurimer's expression was skeptical. "So, do you want to leave a message for Peter?"

"Well, maybe I could drop back later—or he can call me," Esther said.

"I hope you're in no hurry. He's out on the boat."

"A bit late for that, isn't it?" Esther said. "It was chilly along the water this morning."

"You know men—the new toy. He was going to put her in last week and then the forecast said more warm weather and he put it off. After Angela called, the first thing he said was, 'I think I'll go sailing.' He was off like a shot."

"What time was that?" I asked.

"Around eight-thirty, quarter to nine. Why?"

"I just wondered if he might be back this afternoon."

"Late," she said. "He won't be back until it's too late to do anything useful."

"Yes. Well, ask him to call me, please," Esther said. "Are the children well?"

"Darren's had a cold, but the girls are fine. Aren't you, Jackie?" She ruffled the toddler's hair, and the child took her finger out of her mouth and nodded vigorously.

Esther smiled and waved at Jackie. "Bye-bye."

"Say good-bye," her mother prompted, and Jackie gave us the shortest, softest "bye" possible.

On the way back to the car, Esther sighed in exasperation. "Peter has every good gift but sense," she said. "He's really got a nice family. The oldest girl is talented, too. They've started her on one of those little violins."

"But Mrs. is left to cope?"

"Pretty much. And, of course, she lets him know it."

"With reason."

"Very much so, but maybe not the best way to handle him."

"She lacks—the touch of the poet?" I asked as I started the car.

"I'm afraid that's it exactly," Esther said. "I suppose he thought she'd manage everything for him—which she does—and take care of him and the house and the kids. He's spoiled. I knew his parents years ago when he was the musical boy wonder. He's never adjusted to adult life."

"Ah," I said, thinking again of Angela.

"Still, he's a good teacher." Esther was rigorously fair. "Very good. And very professional. There's never been any complaint or anything like that."

"Until now."

"I'm sure there's some explanation. I'm really sorry I dragged you all this way."

"I didn't mean the money. You know that. I meant Angela."

There was a long and pregnant silence from Esther.

"He's in love with her," I continued. "I thought maybe he was just fooling around, but now I think—"

"Peter would be serious," she interrupted. "He's a serious person. Not a bad man, at all, but—I don't know—I've gotten the feeling lately that ordinary life doesn't have what he needs."

"That seems all too common around Branch Hill."

"We had the oddest conversation just before the last concert. I'd come early for the dress rehearsal, and Peter came in and began talking about the soul, about the belief in the soul in the seventeenth century, about how it has its own code. He said a belief in the after-life made all the difference in the way men act."

"What sort of difference?"

"I think he meant the possibility for happiness after death. He said the seventeenth century knew what was serious—the soul, love, God, and redemption."

"The love of God?"

"We think alike," she said. "I asked just that and do you know what he said?"

I shook my head.

"He said, 'All true love touches the soul.' I think he's a very unhappy man."

"I'm suddenly glad Angela is safe at the hospital. I don't like all this love and death and souls in the afterlife. I can't think of a less wholesome atmosphere for a girl of fourteen."

"Or for Peter," Esther said. "I'm a bit worried, but I really didn't know what to say to Jill."

She returned to this idea when I dropped her off at home, and I said, "Call me if you want. After you've gotten in touch with Peter."

"That's kind of you, but I'm sure things will work out."

We left it at that, and I drove into town to see Branch Hill's finest. Lieutenant Canelli was out, and given our previous interview, I was just as glad to draw his partner Burt Wilson of the lacquered hair, black boots, and snappy ties. This morning Wilson looked tired. His hair was not quite as perfect as usual, and a handsome silk floral tie hung limply over the back of his chair.

"What can I do for you?" he asked. He had a coffee cup in one hand and a small box of donuts open on his desk. Breakfast, I guessed, after an all-nighter with the Greene-Browning accident.

"I heard about the accident Ken Browning had last night. They'd given me a lift earlier in the evening when my car broke down."

Wilson pulled over a piece of paper and began taking notes. I recounted our ride to The Lobsterman and the unpleasantness that had led to my departure.

"She drinking?" Wilson asked when I was finished.

"Maybe half a glass of wine."

"And after you left?"

"She couldn't have had time for much more. My cab arrived a couple minutes after I went out to the parking lot. As we left, I saw Miriam and Ken come outside. Arm in arm."

"People are funny," Wilson said.

"Ken's hand—were you able to check with his doctor?"

"Yes. His hands were badly bruised, consistent with dropping a car hood on them."

"Or pounding someone around?"

"That too, unfortunately."

"Miriam Greene wanted some photos back from William Brighton. She claims they were of her pets."

"We've gone through the lot," Wilson said. "Nothing incriminating."

"Do you suppose he lied to her?"

"Brighton, you mean?"

"Yes. He might have been pulling her leg."

"Could be," Wilson said, getting wearily to his feet. "I don't think I'd fool around with that lady."

I waited.

"She managed to just about shear off the passenger side and still walk away without a scratch."

"She was wearing her seat belt?"

"Oh, yes. Unlike Mr. Browning. Sometimes I think we're wasting our breath on warnings—"

"Ken wasn't wearing his belt? You're sure the rescue squad didn't unfasten him?"

"They take note. And we had an officer on the scene. What's the matter?"

"Ken normally wore his seat belt. He had it on last night when they picked me up. And the other day, the day he supposedly hurt his hand, I met him at the station and gave him a ride home. He put his belt on. I know, because I had to help him with the catch."

"You said he was drunk at The Lobsterman."

"And belligerent. But he and Miriam came out together, nonetheless. She fastened her belt. He would have needed help. I just wonder—"

Burt Wilson's face had assumed a sour expression. "So do I," he said.

"WHEN ARE YOU coming back?" my husband asked.

"Soon. Alex has decided to terminate my services."

"Catch the train," Harry said.

"Listen, something odd has happened." I told him about the accident and the Madrigal Society's account.

"So where is this guy?"

"Off sailing his boat as of this morning."

"He won't get too far that way."

"No, I guess not. I'll see about Monday, all right?"

I checked on Harry's diet again and fussed long distance. When I hung up, I called Amtrak and made reservations, checking Sunday as well as Monday trains. It really was not my worry anymore. Since Esther hadn't called, Laurimer must have come back with a reasonable explanation. Ken was out of commission, and Miriam had attracted Burt Wilson's interest. Angela—Angela would have to show some of her precocious talent and look after herself. I went to bed early with sensible thoughts, which was just as well, because the phone rang before it was full light. My heart jumped—Harry wasn't well, he'd had another attack, Jan was calling from the hospital. When I picked up the receiver and said, "Hello," my voice rattled like gravel.

"Anna? It's Esther Reed. I'm sorry to call so early, but he's not back. Hasn't been home all night. Jill's frantic."

I could feel my heart shifting back into its normal gear. "Peter's been out all night in the boat?"

"Jill just called. She's had to notify the Coast Guard."

"I see." But really I didn't. "Was it stormy last night? High wind?"

"No. I called and checked. Although the currents can be bad on the Sound, especially around the islands. He could have had some equipment failure, I suppose."

"Yes."

"I was planning to go flying this morning anyway. I thought I'd go out over the Sound. The Coast Guard will be looking, but an extra pair of eyes might—"

"Shall I come?"

"Pick me up in forty-five minutes," she said and hung up.

ESTHER'S PLANE was implausibly small. My first thought was that it was a toy or a model, and the fact that she easily pulled it from its spot in the hangar and towed it outside did not increase my confidence.

"Do you get airsick?" she asked.

"Not normally."

"You'll like this," Esther said, patting the fuselage with pride. "This is what flying's all about. Skill and response."

I peered into the cockpit and saw a wall of dials. "How do you see out?"

"You don't really. You can see over the top and around the sides. You need to watch your altitude and speed and do the rest by feel. It's a bit like backing up in a car at seventy miles an hour."

This prospect did not seem to faze her, and she walked around the plane, checking the fuel and the oil and running her hand up and down the sleek propeller. "Climb in," she said. "This is an Aeronca Champ, she's prop started. You can help by keeping the brakes on."

"Something I can do with conviction," I said. I clambered over the side and into the back seat, which was narrow, hard, and cold. There was, I noticed, less than a quarter inch of plywood between me and the outside. Esther got in front and began flipping switches. "When we're in the air, we'll use the headsets," she said. "I have a voice-activated intercom—otherwise you wouldn't hear me over the sound of the engine." When she was satisfied that everything was in order, she showed me the brakes and the ignition switches. "They're off now. Down position. When I say, 'Switches hot,' you flick them up. Not before. Okay?"

"Okay."

Esther pushed a fat button that looked like a snow-blower primer, then climbed out and went around to the propeller. She turned the blades several times, then stopped and said, "Switches hot."

I flipped them up. "Switches up—hot."

Esther stepped forward, then in one motion, pulled down on the blade and spun away from the propeller, which came to sudden, noisy, and dangerous life. She pulled herself into the plane and gestured for me to put on my headset.

"Branch Hill traffic, this is Aeronca Champ, nine six eight Kilo Bravo, backtaxiing runway eighteen." There was no answer; the sky was clear.

"…straight out departure on eighteen," Esther said as she turned into the wind and revved the engine. I felt her slip the brake, then the trees raced toward us and we lurched into the air, jumping high-tension wires, a highway, a pond. I had a moment's apprehension that was almost immediately replaced by excitement. Even small commuter planes didn't fly this low. This was bird height, witch height, fantasy gliding. Just below the stubby silver wings, I could see the thick canopy of trees, the small pools and patios, the

garages and hidden gardens, the clothes on the lines,
the upturned faces of surprised children: unexpected
snapshots of lives in progress. At the river, we turned
east into a wall of yellow sun. Below us were gulls
and cormorants, coasting downstream on stiff, out-
stretched wings, a few barges, and little red buoys
bouncing in the tide. The Sound lay ahead, silver and
gray and paved with delicate ripples like the scales
of a giant fish. It was edged with greenish shallows
bearing a few small boats, and with a white shore
that turned rocky as Esther veered northeast before
swinging out across the water.

"Fisher's Island," she said and pointed below.

I saw a green, irregular silhouette, long and thin like
a dragon in the water. As we circled the island, I asked,
"Would he have gone out to sea?"

Esther shrugged. "It depends what he had in
mind," she said.

I didn't ask if she had a theory. Mine was that Peter and Angela had something going. But she was
home, and Peter was missing, and the water, dotted
now with occasional whitecaps, showed no trace of a
small sailing vessel. Block Island lay farther to the
north and east, and Esther indicated her intention to
circle it, then head back. We were gliding along the
seaward side when she suddenly pointed below. There
was a boat on the water, a tiny sailboat with a bare
mast, bobbing quite far out.

"I'm sure that's Peter's," Esther said, dropping us
a little lower. "That's Peter's boat, all right."

"Is the beach shallow? He looks awfully far off
shore."

"Too far out. I'd guess she's been drifting."

We circled again. The deck of Peter's boat was empty.

Esther fiddled with her radio and called the Coast Guard. She talked to a Rhode Island station and then to a Coast Guard ship that we saw on the north side of the island. "They'll take it in tow," she said, when she'd switched off the radio. "If Peter's not on it."

"It certainly looked deserted," I said.

On the way back, Esther was silent and seemed thoughtful.

"You'd mentioned Peter was depressed," I said when the plane's motor was off, and we sat in the expanding silence near the hangar.

"Yes. But no, that wasn't what I was thinking about. It's probable, of course, that he—fell overboard or something—but I was thinking that the boat looked awfully near where the older Laurimers had their summer place."

"Had or still have?"

"Still," she said, "though it's rented out now every summer."

"The police will have to know."

"I expect Jill will mention it," Esther said.

EIGHTEEN

THE MADRIGAL SOCIETY held its regular meeting Sunday night in the St. George's parish hall. Esther, I know, would have preferred to postpone it, but there were so many rumors she decided that a meeting with all its potential awkwardness was preferable to continued speculation. I was present, in part because of the casual arrangements of the society and in part because I now knew as much or more than anyone else about its affairs. My own reasons were obvious: I wanted to see how the various members reacted to Peter Laurimer's disappearance—and to the loss of most of the group's funds.

As treasurer, Esther ran the meeting. She gave a brief synopsis of events, running from her arrival at the local bank with the concert proceeds through our flight over the islands, and concluded with the Coast Guard report on Peter's little sloop, *Poppea,* which had been found, intact but adrift, without any sign of violence or foul play and with its inflatable raft properly stowed.

"Did he fall overboard?" one of the men asked.

"That's apparently the best possibility," Esther said. "The main sail had been lowered, but hadn't been completely fastened. The Coast Guard said the boom was loose. Peter'd apparently been wearing his vest but not his safety harness. It looks as if he might have been working on the sail and been knocked over when the boom swung round."

"He wasn't a good swimmer," Angela said then. "At the picnic last year, remember? He said he was kind of afraid in the water."

Everyone turned to look at her, and Miriam, who had arrived all in black with a black lace scarf—"like the chief mourner," Esther had said tartly—sniffled ostentatiously. Angela, for her part, looked pale and serious but oddly detached, and I couldn't decide whether this confirmed or overturned my assessment. Certainly the leading voices could not have reacted more differently. Miriam seemed devastated, but she expressed this with grandiose plans for funeral music, a memorial concert, and floral tributes, all the while declaring herself nearly prostrate. There was something exaggerated about Miriam, almost unbalanced, but I felt her shock and grief were real. Angela's true feelings were impossible to guess, although I noticed she showed a certain amount of interest in the missing funds. This matter, however, was not explored at length. Esther could report only that they had not been transferred to Laurimer's personal account but had been taken in cash. To do the Society credit, its members seemed more concerned, at least initially, with the human than with the financial loss.

"I hope that will continue," Esther said to me as I drove her home. "Jill is going to have a hard enough time as it is."

"I wonder if he was insured."

"I expect so. I hope so. Of course, the insurance people might drag their feet unless his body is found."

"If he drowned, something will be found sooner or later, won't it?"

"Probably. But it could be much later, and with the three children—I suppose the Laurimers may help out.

I don't know how well fixed Jill's parents are. It's an awful mess."

"You're going to have to mention the Society money to her," I said.

Esther looked uncomfortable.

"You can't expect it to be kept a secret. And there may be a perfectly reasonable explanation."

"Yes, that's true."

"Or are you thinking like me?" I asked.

"You'd better tell me what you mean."

"I mean that Peter's decamped with the Society money. That he left the boat, that he got himself to the island and has even now left town."

"Why would he do that?"

"To protect his family. To enable them to collect on any insurance."

"It's possible, but it's so..." She shrugged.

"You said yourself he seemed unhappy and depressed. If I'm right, he was in love with Angela. We both know he was pursued by Miriam. From what you've said, his marriage was not ideal. He could at least buy a plane ticket courtesy of the Madrigal Society. He may even plan to come back. People do such strange things."

"If you're right, what about Angela?"

"I don't know. She's been frightened, nervous. I know she was pressuring him to do something."

Esther looked at me.

"I overheard them quite by accident the night of the concert. I was wandering around the back of the church when they came out one of the rear doors and started talking. She was very upset about William. Peter kept saying that everything was almost ready. That sort of thing."

"Maybe Ken's accident put an end to it," Esther said. "And maybe this was all just an accident, too." She seemed suddenly annoyed. "Besides, you heard Angela. Peter couldn't swim well. I know that for a fact, and even with a life jacket, the water is rough and dangerous—and cold this time of year, especially once you get off shore."

"There are always possibilities. He could have had—"

"I think we'll leave all that for the police," Esther said brusquely.

We drove the rest of the way in silence, while I tried to retrieve the idea that had surfaced for an instant when I'd mentioned Peter and other possibilities. What else could Peter have had? What else could he have done? There was something I'd seen, something definite, but whatever it was had retired to the mental depths and refused to be recalled.

"Thanks for the ride," Esther said.

"Anytime."

"I really think things need to be left to the police now," she said.

I smiled noncommittally and headed toward the Laurimers' house.

Without the orangey glare of city lights, Branch Hill seemed dark and secretive. There was a pinky urban glow in the sky, all right, but on the ground the voluptuous plantings of suburbia took over. The yards were fronted by big trees that shadowed the grass and sidewalks. The fancier neighborhoods featured spotlights playing on the shrubbery and brightly lit facades, but the Laurimers' property wasn't in the showcase class. Their long, narrow yard was dark except for the streetlight beyond a clump of conifers, and its light was insufficient to keep me from cracking my leg on an overturned tricycle. I was more careful after that, negotiating the sandbox with care and only stumbling once on the porch steps. Although I could see lights upstairs, the lower floor was dark, and it took a while before I heard someone coming downstairs to open the door.

"Yes?" She was slim with olive skin and shoulder-length black hair.

"My name is Anna Peters. I'd like to speak to Jill Laurimer. I met her the other day with Esther Reed."

The woman hesitated. "Jill's pretty upset. This isn't a good time."

I took out one of my cards. "I've been here investigating the Urson murder case. I was with Esther Reed when she spotted Peter's boat. There's something I think Jill could tell me quickly."

"Just a minute," she said and closed the door in my face. I heard her slide the bolt and go upstairs. Then a light went on and then another and Jill Laurimer opened the door.

"It's late," she said. "I'd decided to go to bed early."

"I don't blame you. I'm sorry to intrude, but—"

"No you're not," Jill said. "But I've got some questions to ask you, too."

I stepped into the hallway, and she turned and walked into the kitchen, switching on a bluish fluorescent light when she passed the sink. She'd aged ten years in as many hours, and she looked tired, angry, and determined. She leaned against the counter, crossed her arms and asked, "What was this morning about?"

"With Esther? I should let her—"

"Esther is the soul of discretion."

"You may be glad of that," I said. "It seems there's some money missing from the Society account. Quite a lot of money. Esther and your husband are the only people authorized to make withdrawals. She naturally wondered what had happened and as treasurer—"

"You're as bad as Esther. What's 'quite a lot of money'?"

"Around seven hundred dollars."

Jill Laurimer gave a short, bitter laugh, then wiped her eyes. "Christ! Seven hundred dollars! That's Peter! What the hell are you bothering me with that for? That's not enough to pay a month's bills!"

"I never supposed he took it—if he took it—to pay off household bills."

"No?"

I shook my head and she came over to the kitchen table and sat down. I took another chair. "Your husband," I said carefully, "seemed very fond of Angela Browning. He told me she was the best student he was ever likely to have."

"Angela Browning is a little bitch. And that Greene woman is another one."

"And neither is very fond of the other."

"That's the only good thing I can say about either one of them."

"Was Peter—serious—about either one?"

"Was he screwing them, you mean?" She looked bitterly unhappy.

"That doesn't necessarily mean he was serious."

"Serious! You know, I always thought I understood Peter. Peter was serious about music. I understood that. He was serious about music, and I was

serious about him. He expected to do great things.
Maybe I expected that, too: first nights, Tanglewood,
European engagements. I could have lived with that."

"Great things are hard to do in the arts. And not
necessarily quickly done, either."

She shook her head. "Musicians, musicians de-
velop fast or not at all. You have to be awfully good,
awfully early."

"And Peter?"

"Good. Maybe awfully good, I don't know anymore. Talent isn't enough. You need luck and con-
tacts and drive. Drive and ambition maybe most of
all." She ran one hand through her hair and looked
down at the table. "Peter's unworldly. He's on another planet."

"Esther says he lives in the seventeenth century."

"Yeah—anywhere but here and now. He can be
fun, you know. He's great with the kids. God! I don't
know what to tell the kids. Or whether to tell them yet.
Jackie's been asking. She knows he went out on the
boat, because he went into her room early to say good-
bye."

"Did he usually do that?"

Jill Laurimer shrugged her shoulders. "It was never
important before."

"No."

There was a long silence in which she got up and put
on some coffee. "You don't have much to say," she
said.

"I only have the one question. That'll tell me—"

"What?"

"If we have a chance he's alive."

Suspicious of hope, Jill took a deep breath. "The
Coast Guard says it looks as if he fell overboard."

"I know. I was with Esther in the plane when we spotted the boat. She talked to them then and later, too. But there's no proof without a body."

"He had an affair with Miriam last winter," Jill said abruptly. "Out of the blue. Early mid-life crisis, I thought."

"Not typical behavior?"

"No. I can say that confidently. Peter's not very adept at concealing things. I knew right away."

"And put a stop to it?"

"More or less. I should have been suspicious about that."

"Why?"

"Because I think it was Angela from the first. Miriam was just a diversion. I think he went to bed with her to keep away from Angela. I really do."

"Did Miriam know that?"

"She's certainly not stupid. Sooner or later."

"How did she react, do you know?"

"Like the hypocrite she is. Smiles on the outside, combined with ruthless maneuvering. Miriam's just got to have her own way. That was what I couldn't stand. I just couldn't let it alone. I told Peter it had to stop and it did. Miriam was ripped. You know, she'd practically made herself over for Peter. I suppose I should have been flattered."

"I heard she'd lost weight."

"Lost weight, changed her hair, got a whole new wardrobe—all very severe and grand."

"And Angela? When did she come into the picture, romantically, I mean?"

"Just lately, I think. Christ! Men are so stupid! Peter was absolutely fascinated by her. She was 'the most gifted singer, the most wonderful student.' She had 'the spirit of the period, a real seventeenth-century soul'—all that nonsense. What she does have is Peter's talent for period music combined with a really first-rate voice. In addition to everything else, she was his second chance at a big career.''

"I'm interested in the timing. Since the Urson killing?"

"I'd say, sometime before. I should have wrung her neck. I should have slapped her smug little face and gone to her parents, but I have my own kids to think about, and though Peter doesn't make a lot of money, he makes a lot more than I could. And then, I wasn't sure—Peter isn't your ordinary child molester, you know. She was after him, tooth and nail—like Miriam.'' She shook her head. "He's so damn idealistic. I think it would have suited him to have an 'untouchable lady'.''

"Very poetic.''

"Very unrealistic. In the seventeenth century, people locked up their daughters. It was a whole lot easier to keep things platonic.

"Hence Miriam.''

"I should have ignored Miriam, that's what I should have done. She'd have gotten tired of him, like all her others. Angela would have been disgusted and Peter would have been disillusioned. I really blew it.''

"We can't always be sufficiently calculating.''

"No.''

"And Angela's side of things?'' I asked. "What's your estimate? Childish crush or something more?''

"She's a child. Of course it was infatuation.'' Jill looked uncomfortable. I guessed she was good with children, and that the children, not Peter, had always been her priority. She looked away. "To tell you the honest truth, he was good for her. She was a pathetic little thing in spite of the talent, the looks. Like a blank slate. No one cared much about her at home except Martha. Martha's the only one she ever mentioned, in fact. I always had the feeling there was nothing there— and then she started singing with Peter, and he started writing on the slate and she became weird and beautiful.''

"Weird?"

"You know how she is, unnaturally sophisticated and grown up. Weird—she's like something out of Shakespeare or earlier. She wants to be Juliet or Heloise; she wants to die for love. It's quite unbelievable, all those gloomy songs, but that's why she sings them so convincingly. Peter gave her this whole outlook, this whole antique moral code, and now she's like a visitor from another time.''

"Peter's time?"

"Peter's looking to escape," she said.

"That's my theory. His boat—it came equipped with safety equipment?"

"Oh sure, life vests for everyone. Well, the children didn't often go—they're too young, sailing is boring for them, but I sometimes went. Life vests and a safety harness for when he's on the boat alone, and one of those orange rubber lifeboat things.''

"His was still on board.''

"That's right. He fell over and I hope to God they find him soon, one way or the other. Except for the kids, I wouldn't much care which, after what he's put me through.''

"There's one more thing. You do know where his boat was found?''

"Off Block Island. The Coast Guard guy went over all that."

"Esther told me it was near where his parents have a house. I don't want to raise your hopes, but I think he could still be alive."

Jill Laurimer shook her head. "I know what you're thinking, but he wouldn't have gone without Angela. He'd have left the rest of us," she said bitterly, "but he wouldn't have gone without her."

NINETEEN

IT WAS WET Monday morning, cold and rather blustery. I was out early. I'd decided to go home, and I just had time to buy Harry a present and to stop by Alex Valon's before I caught the train. If I felt a certain dissatisfaction with leaving a job undone, I wasn't the only one. Like Branch Hill's finest, I had come up against ambiguity and good alibis. I'd been handsomely paid for shifting the detective squad's attention from Scott Cushing to Ken and Miriam. Beyond that, I had nothing to offer but theories, and even those came up against the oddities of the case: Ken was supposedly in the clear for the Urson death, and Miriam, for both, and yet...

I was outside the sporting-goods store when I stopped abruptly, disconcerting the man who was walking behind me. "Sorry," I said and peered into the window. As befitting Branch Hill's dual identity as wealthy playground and beach resort, the windows were divided between costly tennis, squash, and ski gear, and nautical supplies. Representative of the latter, and just visible behind a mass of rubberized foul-weather clothing, was a large yellow rubber raft. I remembered the day I'd taken Angela to lunch. She had hurried out afterwards, crossed the street to the mall and reappeared a moment later with Peter Laurimer, who, I now remembered, had been carrying a very large and awkward-looking parcel. I opened the sports shop door and went inside, perhaps the first of the day's customers, because the young clerk approached immediately.

"I'm thinking about buying a rubber life raft—for my husband's boat."

"What size?"

"Well, I don't know. I think it was Peter Laurimer who told me he'd gotten a good price on one from you not too long ago."

The clerk turned and called into the back. "Meg, did we sell a rubber raft to Mr. Laurimer?"

A short woman with neat gray hair and a bright expression came out of the back. "What can I help you with?" she asked.

I explained I was looking for a rubber raft and that I'd admired one Peter Laurimer had gotten.

"Oh, yes. That was during our sale. But those were the black ones. For a boat we'd recommend one of the yellow or orange ones. Much more visible."

"Peter'd seemed satisfied," I said, trying to sound doubtful.

"He wanted one for his kids when they went to the lake. For his boat, he has an orange one. We sold him that one, too. First quality. Poor Mr. Laurimer. I feel sick about him."

"It's awful," I agreed.

"Now we have small rafts in stock," the clerk said, recovering his professional aplomb. "Twelve feet and up, we'd have to order for you."

"Oh, that's too bad," I said. "I'm leaving today. I'll have to think of something else."

I thanked them and left. I called Jill Laurimer from the first phone I saw: She hadn't noticed a second raft and the kids never went near any lake that she knew of. The police would be interested in that, but I decided to get Harry's print first while I was still in the center.

Although it only took me a few minutes to select one, the clerk was painfully slow with the packaging, and when I rushed out of the shop with my purchase, I just missed colliding with Miriam Greene. She was striding toward the mall exit, looking smart, happy, and triumphant. She was wearing a beautiful deep violet wool dress with a fox wrap, extraordinary purple suede heels, and a quite magnificent necklace and earrings of amethysts set in gold. She was carrying a lightweight case and a purple suede bag, and my heart lifted when I saw that she was going traveling.

"Oh, hello, Anna. How nice to see you! I'd heard you were on your way home."

"Soon," I said.

"You've had an eventful trip."

"Yes. I must say you're looking well. After the accident and all."

"Disaster. Just disaster. I could hardly breathe for days."

She looked to be breathing just fine at the moment. "A terrible shock," I said.

"Terrible. And poor Ken. Of course, he's just unmanageable when he's drunk—he wouldn't hear of a seat belt."

"There's some hope . . ."

"Oh, yes. He'll be all right. They think his memory was affected. But Ken's was never too reliable." She smiled then, a radiantly egotistical smile. "I've got to run. Lovely to have seen you." She paused a moment at the door to put up a violet umbrella. As I followed her down the street, I could see it bobbing in the crowd. The airport? The train station? Or a rendez-

vous somewhere—perhaps with Peter? I decided that
certainty was worth something; Amtrak would have to
wait. I loitered beside an odiferous garbage hauler in
the municipal lot until I saw her get into a black
Honda, then sprinted to my rental and managed the
exit in time to see her turn onto the main street, away
from the water.

I followed her to the interstate. Miriam turned north
and drove fast through the last of the morning commuter traffic, which thickened so much near New
London that I almost lost her at the business district,
and I was in the wrong lane for the abrupt turn she
made into the Amtrak station. I saw a parking area
ahead, took the first spot, and ran across the road.
The black Honda was not in the temporary parking
area in front of the station, and, as the tracks and the
river were directly behind the building, I could not at
first see where she had gone. Then a car swung in behind me and turned sharply to the right, across a
boardwalk and onto a dock. The car ferry to Block
Island was in port and loading. I'd guessed right, after all.

At the ticket booth, I was told that the ferry already had its full load of cars, but when I learned that
the crossing took two and a half hours, I stopped
worrying. I found a phone in the station and called
Esther Reed. She was annoyed with me for talking to
Jill Laurimer, but the idea that Miriam was off to
rainy Block Island in full regalia struck her as odd.
Odd enough so that she agreed to meet me at the Groton airport and take me to the island.

After I hung up, I called Harry, Amtrak, and the car
rental, then drove to the airport, which was bigger and
more impressive than Branch Hill's and also foggier.

White wisps of mist rose all along the river, and by the time Esther arrived, she was lucky to land safely. When I walked toward the plane, I saw her shake her head.

"Bad?"

"Terrible and getting worse. They'll be closing everything. You'll have to take the boat."

"They don't run many after Labor Day—that was the last outbound."

"Well," said Esther, "we'll have to wait until the weather clears."

We went into Groton for coffee, then drove on to New London where I met the inbound ferry in late afternoon to be sure that Miriam hadn't returned. We ate dinner at a nearby restaurant, and by the time we came out, the temperature had dropped sharply. Esther phoned to find accommodation on the island, and by eleven the fog had lifted enough for us to take off across the wide dark of the Sound.

WE DIDN'T FIND Peter that night, and although we located Miriam's hotel, the desk clerk said she was out. Her black Honda had still not arrived in the parking lot when I gave up at one A.M. I was up again at seven, and at ten minutes to eight, Esther and I were headed north toward the Laurimers' old summer house. It was a gray, raw morning that matched my mood.

"We probably should talk to the neighbors," Esther said. "If we're going to be poking around the Laurimers'."

"How close are the neighbors?" I asked.

"Just down the road."

"Out of sight, we won't worry about them."

"I really think—" Esther began, but I said, "We haven't time. I think they'll try for the ferry this morning. Once they're in New London, they can drive into New York or take the train and just disappear."

"Why did she meet him?" Esther asked.

"I don't know. And why her? I was betting everything on Angela. I still am. Even Ken mentioned that Miriam hadn't a chance with Laurimer."

"Miriam doesn't know the meaning of defeat."

"But how did she know? That's the other thing. She was genuinely upset when the boat was found. Didn't you think so?"

"There's the turn," Esther said. "It's just a track. Yes, I thought so. More upset than Angela, although perhaps Angela has just reverted."

"Reverted?"

"That's how she was when she first joined the group. Very detached, very distant and cool."

"The thing of it is, Miriam seemed completely different yesterday—cheerful, more than cheerful, victorious. My guess is that she knew something she didn't know before."

"Which means Peter—or someone—got in touch with her."

"That's my assumption," I said as I stopped the car near the edge of the Laurimers' property.

"You can drive right up. There's room to park in the yard."

"I don't want to spoil any tracks," I said. "Maybe we'll be able to tell if Peter's had company."

The dirt drive was scored by ruts, some obviously old. "I wish we knew when the summer tenants left."

"These are fresh," Esther said, nodding toward the lawn. "Somebody drove right up the back."

There was a dark, shingled barn fitted out as a garage with overhead doors, and someone had driven beyond it to a dilapidated shed. Esther lifted the lid of a garbage can by the barn. "Look at this." She pointed to some new looking soup cans and candy wrappers.

I tried the overhead doors, but those, like the small side entrance, were locked. Esther, uneasy about all this snooping, insisted on going back to try the house. While she was tapping on the shuttered windows and ringing the bell, I found an old piece of wire and managed to jimmy the barn door.

Inside was cold and rather damp, with a smell of earth, whitewash, and hay as faint as nostalgia. I detected, too, an odor of bottled gas that conjured memories of old camp stoves and half-forgotten picnics: Someone had been cooking in the barn. I climbed up to the loft and checked the rafters for Peter's black rubber boat, without success. Esther was down on the main floor of the barn, where once they'd have kept machines and excess bales of hay. She had opened one of the overhead doors from the inside and, in the soft island light, was inspecting something in one corner.

"Someone's been digging," she said, and pointed to a shovel streaked with earth.

"Summer gardener?"

Esther shrugged. "I didn't see any flower beds."

"Let's look in the other barn," I suggested, and this time she did not fuss about trespassing.

We followed the tire tracks back to the shed. Its wobbly sliding door ran on a sagging track, and once we'd pushed it open, we realized that the car, whosever it was, had been parked inside. We could see the marks in the dirt floor. This building was in far worse repair than the main barn and, although it was probably a better place to hide a car, the choice made me uneasy. I had difficulty imagining Miriam, immaculately and beautifully dressed, vivid with all her dangerous energy and ambition, in the damp and gloomy shed. I think Esther had similar misgivings, because she was looking around apprehensively.

Outside were the remains of a small fenced paddock, and then a patch of shrub and small trees. I don't know what made me walk back through the rutted field and into the scrub—perhaps the symmetry with the grove in the Estates.

It was damp underfoot and downright wet in even the slightest depression, with a great odor of humus and fallen leaves. I did not go far, maybe a hundred yards in all—though farther, I thought, than Miriam ever would have strolled in those high violet suede heels—before I heard Esther calling. She was pointing to her watch, and a glance of mine showed ten of nine—we would miss the ferry departure. I turned and started back down through the trees, saw a glimmer in the leaves, and stopped: a bit of broken glass? A child's bauble? My heart jumped nonetheless. I bent down, brushed away some leaves, and picked up one of Miriam's gold and amethyst earrings.

"We'll be late," Esther said when I reached her. Then she looked at me closely. "What's the matter?"

"We may be too late," I said.

"Not if we hurry."

I shook my head. "Even last night may have been too late. Look."

"It's very pretty," Esther said.

"Don't you recognize it?"

"No. But then I never notice jewelry."

"Miriam was wearing a pair of these when I saw her in town yesterday. She's definitely been here."

"She could have dropped it. People are always losing—"

"Up there? I can't see Miriam walking up through the weeds in the rain, can you?"

"No," said Esther quickly. "No, but let's hurry. We may still make the boat."

WE MISSED THE FERRY by minutes. Someone else had been more fortunate, for Miriam's Honda had reappeared in the parking lot at the dock. Esther looked very serious and agreed to fly back to Groton immediately. From there, we drove into New London and reached the dock shortly before the ferry was due. After I parked the car, I asked Esther to watch the slip and to call the police if she spotted Peter.

"The moment he lands," I said. "Before you do anything else."

"All right, but where are you going?"

"I'm going to look for Angela," I said.

TWENTY

I FOUND HER IN the Amtrak station, sitting on one of the big wooden benches that faced the tracks and the river. I bought a newspaper and sat down next to her. Angela was studying a musical score, and it was several seconds before she realized that I was there. I heard her catch her breath sharply.

"Have you been waiting long?" I asked, still examining the headlines.

"I'm meeting a friend."

"There will be a train back to Branch Hill soon. You should get on it and forget all this. Really you should," I said.

She looked at me then, her enormous eyes serious. "How could I do that?" she asked. "I've promised."

"He shouldn't have asked you. He should not have asked you to promise anything."

"But I wanted to," she said. "I wanted to more than anything in life."

"You know he's married. He has children of his own."

"He said I was the other half of his soul," Angela said with perfect seriousness.

"If you're not here, he can go back to his wife and family and his job. If nothing else has happened."

"What about me?" she asked then. "He knows I have to get away."

"Why? Why do you have to get away?"

"You know what happened to Lindsay," Angela said. "I was afraid."

"Why?"

"I'm going away and never coming back." She clutched her bag.

"Then it won't matter if you tell me."

There was a long silence.

"Miriam wanted him," she said finally. "So she decided to kill me."

"And?"

"And she killed Lindsay by mistake. I knew that all along."

"And never said?"

"Just to Peter. I finally told him. I had to. You see, she had forgotten Lindsay, and she was thinking about me again."

I was struck by her phrasing: "She had forgotten Lindsay." Possibly that was true, possibly that was the reason Miriam had seemed so blandly innocent. She'd intended to kill Angela or, more likely, she'd been irresistibly tempted by the opportunity of night and shadows. I imagined her out walking her dog and seeing her hated rival alone, and the discarded club and the trees of the grove. Then came a moment's madness before the discovery of error, an error that could make you die of remorse—unless you were fatally self-centered like Miriam, who erased her crime as an accident, as something that never was.

"And William?" I asked "Did William know?"

"I think William guessed," she said. "He knew she went out walking every night. He knew she sometimes met one of her boyfriends in the grove. He had a picture of her and some man there."

"And tried to blackmail Miriam with it?"

"She wanted the negative," Angela said. "I suppose she thought it might give people ideas. But she deserved to pay. Like blood guilt. She deserved to pay, don't you think?"

"And your father?"

"She tried to kill him, too," Angela said.

"Your father went to get the negative back for her?"

"I don't know," Angela said, her voice rising. "I didn't know about that. We're just kids! We aren't supposed to have to know everything!"

"How did you know to come today?" I asked.

"Peter and I planned that. We've been waiting for the right time."

"What was the 'right time'?"

"After the concerts—when there'd be enough money. We'd planned to wait until one more. Then there was the accident, and I was afraid and I said we'd have to do it right away."

So it had been money, the enemy of romance, after all. Angela had no resources and Peter had gone to the bank too early to get enough. In mad simplicity, he must have thought of asking Miriam for a loan; he would have been safer robbing the bank.

"You know it's impossible now," I said. "You must understand that."

"No! We're going away! Today! By tonight we'll be far away. You'll see," she said, getting up in agitation and going over to the window. She glanced up and down the platform, then raced to the door and outside toward Peter Laurimer. He flung his arms around her, but when he saw me come out, he released her and stepped back a little. I saw Angela shaking her head.

"It doesn't make any difference," she said, but Peter had gone very pale.

"Everyone will be relieved," I said, "to know you are safe."

"They don't need to know," Angela said. "Please! They don't need to know."

"It would be better for my family," he said, "if you could keep a secret."

He was as innocent as Angela, I saw, but with less reason. "I don't like to lie to people," I said. "Least of all to children."

"We have no other choice," Peter said. "This is our only chance."

"Perhaps," I said. "Unless something's happened to Miriam. Where is she?"

"Miriam?" He swallowed hard but smiled. "At home, I suppose."

I shook my head. "She went over to the island yesterday."

Angela looked surprised; Peter looked like a ghost. "I didn't know that," he said.

"The train's coming!" Angela said. "We've got to go—she can't stop us!"

Peter looked at her sadly, as if he already knew it was too late.

"Come on," she said, touching his arm.

Behind us, the engine slid by, brakes squealed, and the doors of the cars opened.

"We'll be too late!" Angela lifted her case and started toward the train.

"There's really nothing you can do to stop us."

"Peter, come on! Hurry!" Angela cried. "I'm getting on."

"Only this." I reached into my pocket and held out the earring.

Peter closed his eyes and a thin film of sweat appeared on his pallid features.

"Where did you find it?" he asked in a soft, hoarse voice.

"In the scrub," I said. "In the scrub behind your old house."

His face began to close in on itself and to collapse all the youthful lines into age and defeat. "It wasn't deliberate," he said finally. "I didn't mean to hurt her at all."

"But you did?"

"She wouldn't let me go," he said in a querulous voice. "She refused to see reason. To see the reason I had to leave. She said she'd tell everyone. Angela's parents, my wife. And then..."

Behind us, Angela was calling, nervous about the train's departure. "And then?"

He shook his head. "She wouldn't believe I didn't love her. She wouldn't believe that I'd just wanted some money. She couldn't believe that it was all for Angela. She started to take her clothes off. I couldn't stand it. I hit her. I only meant to discourage her. I never meant to hurt her, but you know she had a terrible temper." He sounded surprised, and I felt a moment's pity for Miriam, who had been so wildly and so stupidly misunderstood. "We began struggling, and then—"

"Peter!"

He turned to her in anguish. "It's too late!" he cried. "I can't go now. Miriam's dead!" And then he sat down and put his face in his hands.

IN SIDONIE URSON'S fine living room, the sea light sparkled in the glass and gleamed on the polished floors and whitened the pale walls. I'd promised to tell her and I had. Between what I'd told her and what she'd already heard from Detective Canelli, she knew as much as we were ever likely to know about her daughter's death and its aftermath.

"Three murderers!"

"Two, at least, were manslaughter," I corrected. Ken would almost certainly face nothing more serious, his reputation as a drinker protecting him from the suspicion of premeditation, and his severe injuries provoking sympathy. Peter might face more serious charges. Only those who knew him well would believe him innocent enough to have contemplated borrowing money from Miriam in order to run away with her rival. He should have listened to Angela about Miriam.

"And they all knew," Sidonie said when I was finished. "They all knew."

"They suspected," I said. "Only Miriam knew."

"And Marvin. Marvin was her alibi. He had to know. Jesus! She walked that damn dog every night. Why did we never think of that?"

"Because she was your neighbor," I said. "As for Marvin, he did not want to know." That had been Canelli's theory, and I felt he was right.

"Like Ken and Isabel. That's why she was so solicitous."

"I'm certain she didn't know." Isabel was still under sedation, her tidy life in pieces. I was convinced she'd been ignorant, but who could be sure? And Ken must eventually have had some idea. I thought that was probably why he'd gotten so drunk the night of the concert. According to Canelli, Ken thought that Miriam had been on her way to confirm their meeting that evening. Apparently she often stopped by when she was out with the dog.

"Ken knew," Sidonie said relentlessly, "and William."

"They haven't exactly escaped unharmed."

"No, and in my heart I feel they deserved it. Even Angela. The police questioned her. Why the hell didn't she say something?"

"Angela is a frightened fourteen-year-old, condemned, I'd guess, to years of therapy. What could she have said? 'I think my next-door neighbor intended to kill me, because I'm having an affair with the man she wanted'?"

Sidonie got up and walked over to the splendid windows and looked out to sea. "Of course, if you hadn't come back, Miriam would have gotten away with it. And the rest of them would have kept their mouths shut. That's what I can't accept—our neighbors, our friends. I'll never forgive them for that."

"Miriam would have made a mistake sooner or later. And maybe if I hadn't come along, William would still be alive. I don't know."

"You seem a bit ambivalent," she said, turning to face me. "You could have gone home. I know Alex Valon fired you."

"Don't ruin my reputation. Alex felt I'd done enough to clear Scott."

"That's all he cared about. Nobody cared about Lindsay."

"Except you and Bradley," I said. "Maybe there are never too many people who care about any one of us."

"You have a way of telling people things they never wanted to know," Sidonie said.

"Perhaps that's what makes investigators ambivalent. One can as easily make things worse as better."

"I wanted to know," she said. "And now I do. Thank you for that." She turned to the window again. "I know you have a plane to catch."

"Good-bye," I said. "I am sorry."

But Sidonie was looking out to sea again, out into the bitterness of her loss. The wonderful, bright apartment suddenly seemed claustrophobic. I could not wait to get downstairs and into my car and out onto the highway that led to the airport. When I got there, I dialed Harry's workshop.

"Is everything all right?" he asked. "Aren't you coming home?"

"Yes. My plane goes in fifteen minutes. I just wanted to let you know." Actually, I wanted to tell him I still loved him madly, but I'm always terrible on long distance. Fortunately, Harry can translate.

"I'd better get in the car," he said. "I don't want to be late."

Since his illness, Harry is a lot more concerned about timing, about getting an early start, about not rushing. "I can get a cab if you're tired."

"I've been driving for a while," Harry said. "Ever since you left."

"I'm sorry it's been so long."

"That's okay. It was good for me to start driving again."

"The odd thing is that I shouldn't have had to come back here. I should have known from the beginning. From when Angela told me she thought Lindsay had died of a heart attack. I think that's what it was for each of them—an attack, a momentary madness.''

"Love's a risky business," Harry said.

"Yes."

"But come home anyway. It's dull without you."

The PA started to call my flight, and I thought how lucky we'd been: Harry's heart attack had been a mild one, neither physically nor psychically lethal. We had been fortunate, and although statistics said I'd wind up like Sidonie, contemplating irreparable losses, that time was not yet. On my way out to the plane, I thought I'd be wise to be thankful.

Take 3 books and a surprise gift FREE

SPECIAL LIMITED-TIME OFFER

Mail to: The Mystery Library™
3010 Walden Ave.
P.O. Box 1867
Buffalo, N.Y. 14269-1867

YES! Please send me 3 free books from the Mystery Library™ and my free surprise gift. Then send me 3 mystery books, first time in paperback, every month. Bill me only $3.69 per book plus 25¢ delivery and applicable sales tax, if any*. There is no minimum number of books I must purchase. I can always return a shipment at your expense and cancel my subscription. Even if I never buy another book from the Mystery Library™, the 3 free books and surprise gift are mine to keep forever.   415 BPY ANQ2

Name	(PLEASE PRINT)	
Address		Apt. No.
City	State	Zip

MURDER AT THE CLASS REUNION

TRISS STEIN

A Kay Engels Mystery

First Time in Paperback

CLASS KILLER

After making it "big" as a New York journalist, Kay Engels returns to her twentieth high school reunion, hoping to find a good human interest story.

So when Terry Campbell, voted Best Looking in Her Class, is found strangled in her hotel bed while her classmates danced nearby, Kay's got her story. Terry had always been poison, and age had not impoved her.

As Kay puts her reporter's instincts into police business, she finds romance with the former class bad boy and uncovers a shocking secret in her own past. Then another murder brings her closer to a killer who will give her the story of a lifetime...but she may be too dead to write it.

Available in October at your favorite retail stores.

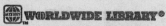 **WORLDWIDE LIBRARY** ®

REUNION